KU-477-182

Ours is a technological age and
SF – as sired by H. G. Wells, or
Jules Verne if you insist – is one
of its offspring.
. . . Is that how you see it ?
You couldn't be more wrong according
to editor I. O. Evans, who has done some
time travelling down the ages and
returned bearing a sparkling collection
of twelve really weird and wonderful
stories:
Among others, a sizzling report on a
no-holds-barred interplanetary war
fought a fantastic two thousand years
ago out there beyond the sun; or, a full
three centuries before that, a highly
sophisticated civilization goes down
to cataclysmic destruction under the
sheer weight of its own scientific
know-how; coming up to time present,
a mere three hundred and odd years ago,
there is an absorbing tale of a mutant
to end all mutants who inhabits an
'oasis' in the Antarctic wastes. . . .
Mr Evans' discoveries are a SF eye-opener

Science Fiction Through the Ages 2, a
round-up of pace-makers in the contemporary
field, will appear shortly

Also by I. O. Evans
in Panther Books

Science Fiction Through the Ages 2

Science Fiction Through the Ages 1

edited by
I. O. Evans

A Panther Book

Science Fiction Through the Ages 1

A Panther Book

First published by
Panther Books Limited 1966

This collection copyright
© I. O. Evans 1966

This book is sold subject to the
condition that it shall not, by way
of trade *or otherwise*, be lent,
re-sold, hired out or otherwise
circulated without the publisher's
prior consent in any form of binding
or cover other than that in which
it is published *and without a similar
condition including this condition
being imposed on the subsequent
purchaser.*

*Printed in Great Britain by Cox & Wyman Ltd.,
London, Reading and Fakenham, and published
by Panther Books Ltd.,
108 Brompton Road, London, S.W.3*

Acknowledgements

Thanks are given to the following publishers
and others for permission to include
copyright extracts in this anthology:
To The Harvard University Press and William
Heinemann for the extract from the translation
by A. M. Harmon in The Loeb Classical
Library of Lucian's *A True Story*.
To Patrick Moore and George G. Harrap &
Co. Ltd., for the extract from Mr Moore's
Science and Fiction.
To Arco Publications for the extract from the
Fitzroy edition of Jules Verne's *Twenty
Thousand Leagues Under the Sea*.

Contents

INTRODUCTION

SCIENCE fiction is not, as is sometimes thought, a recent innovation: it is the modern development of that age-old art-form the 'wonder story'. The hero who amid strange surroundings encounters strange perils and wields strange powers against strange enemies appears throughout world literature. Such narratives, however fantastic they may be, base themselves on contemporary culture, so it is not surprising that the wonder story of the Technical Age should base itself on technics.

Many of the themes of science fiction are traditional. The 'Bug-eyed Monster', or BEM, the fantastic or terrifying creature unknown to the naturalist, made a very early appearance. Odysseus had to brave such perils as the many-headed sea-serpent Scylla and as Charybdis, a creature so voracious that it threatened the mariner by alternately gulping down and vomiting up the sea. Sindbad the Sailor faced more than his fair share of menacing BEMs, including a giant serpent and a beast 'called rhinoceros' so huge that it could impale an elephant on its horn, and he escaped from a snake-infested valley by the ingenious plan of lashing himself to the foot of a roc, a bird even more monstrous than the rhinoceros, for it used elephants to feed its young! Not all such creatures were inimical, however; a wonder story from ancient Egypt describes the encounter of a shipwrecked mariner with a benevolent sea-serpent, gorgeous in blue and gold.

Folk-lore and literature are alike full of such fantasies: were-wolves, mermaids, and sea-serpent, the kraken, the harpies, Cerberus and the centaurs. (These admittedly are not usually regarded as bug-eyed monsters, but that is simply because they are so familiar to our thought; and some, like the unicorn and the dragon, have acquired such mystical overtones that nobody would dream of calling them BEMs.) One such creature may indeed appear, as the so-called 'Apocalyptic Beast', upon the

9

wall of Lascaux Cavern, in southern France.

Among the most fearsome BEMs known to science fiction are the beast-men, the humanoid creatures which figure in folk-lore and literature as the giant, ogre, or troll. Grendel, in the *Beowulf* saga, is an example of these; Odysseus was imprisoned by a man-eating giant, and so was Sindbad, who had also to cope with the 'Old Man of the Sea'.

Regions which might be described by the American term *bad-lands* form the scene of some of these narratives and are even glanced at in the early travel-books. Jason when in quest of the Golden Fleece had his vessel the *Argo* threatened by two 'clashing rocks'; the Greek geographer Pythias heard of a northerly region, Thule, where the sea appeared to be 'curdled' and resembled a 'sea-lung', as though some monster were breathing beneath the waves. St. Brendan likewise reached a 'clogged' sea, in which he sighted a lofty mountain made of crystal.

Here are obvious references to the Arctic, with the moving icebergs and the ice-sludge ground into pulp by the waves. Ingenious attempts have similarly been made to explain Scylla as an octopus and Charybdis as a whirlpool. Sindbad's roc may be a folk-memory of the extinct Aepyornis of Madagascar – really a wingless bird, but why should so trivial a detail be allowed to spoil a good story?

The essential difference between the old-time wonder story and science fiction is that the former is based on magic and the latter on what at any rate purports to be science. Homer's Circe, for example, turns human beings into animals by enchantment; Wells' sinister Dr. Moreau turns animals into humanoid beings by vivisection. Fantastic as are the BEMs, the badlands and achievements of science fiction, they are supposed to be 'natural' in the sense that they are not supernatural. Spells and other enchantments are barred – these belong to another branch of literature, 'fantasy' – as are demons, angels, and the interposition of Providence.

Suggestions of science fiction appear, however, in Scripture. The apocryphal *Book of the Wisdom of Solomon* (Ch. XI, 18–19) refers to creatures that in any other context would be called BEMs:

'Unknown wild beasts full of rage, newly-created, breathing out either a fiery vapour, or filthy scents of scattered smoke, or shooting horrible sparks out of their eyes: Whereof not

only the harm might dispatch [the wicked] at once, but also
the terrible sight utterly destroy them.'

One of the apocryphal Gospels, *The Book of James or the
Protevangelicum* (Ch. XVIII, 2) describes the birth of Christ
as being marked by what is sometimes known in science fiction
as a 'stasis of time', a period during which time literally stands
still.

The term 'science fiction in the Bible' has been applied – I do
not know by whom – to the opening of *The Book of the Prophet
Ezekiel*. An article by Arthur W. Orton* suggests that the 'Four-
Faced Visitors of Ezekiel' may really be space-men whose bizarre
appearance is produced by their helmets and breathing-appar-
atus; helicopteral attachments to their space-suits resemble 'wheels'
when they are revolving and 'wings' when they are at rest.

Remarkable as Mr. Orton's theory is, it is outdistanced by that
of H. S. Bellamy.† He regards *The Book of Revelation* as being
based on records of a former moon which collapsed and showered
the earth with its fragments, and of the 'capture' by the earth's
gravitation of our present moon. Each of these cosmic events
produced catastrophic effects upon the world and its inhabitants,
among them being the destruction of Atlantis.

The Bible apart, it will be seen from the following selection –
which is generally arranged in chronological order – that science
fiction has had a long and honourable history. Among those who
have contributed to it are a classical author, Lucian; a scientist,
Kepler; a 'Utopographer', Francis Bacon; three satirists, Swift,
Voltaire and Samuel Butler; a historical novelist, Walter Scott –
and if the Atlantis tradition has no factual basis but is only an
elaborate myth, a philosopher, Plato. Who can despise an art-
form which can boast such names as these?

The second part of this anthology, dealing with its modern
development, will not attempt the impossible task of covering
the ground completely. Ignoring the more hackneyed themes of
science fiction, it will illustrate some of the more unusual, its
aim being to show how wide and varied is the ground which it
covers.

                                                    I. O. E.

* In *Analog Science Fact-Fiction*, British edition, Vol. XVII,
No. 2, July 1961.
  † *The Book of Revelation is History*.

SECRET WEAPON

WALTER SCOTT

from *Count Robert of Paris*.

Like the bug-eyed monsters and the badlands in the ancient wonder stories, the strange devices and secret weapons that these describe may also have a factual basis. The 'waxen wings' fabricated by Daedalus, like the legendary 'flying horses' and 'flying carpets', may possibly refer to early experiments with gliders or parachutes, and the fall of Daedalus' son Icarus may likewise be founded on fact. Beowulf's magic sword, Arthur's Excalibur, and even the Hammer of Thor, may recall some improvement in the manufacture of weapons, when steel superseded iron, or iron superseded bronze.

One traditional secret weapon seems to be more than a legend, the 'Greek Fire' said to have been used in antiquity but whose nature is unknown. An improved type, invented or re-invented in the seventh century A.D., is stated* to have combined quick-lime with such combustibles as sulphur and naphtha. The mixture would take fire when wetted, nor could its flames be quenched in the ordinary way by drenching it with water.

In his novel *Count Robert of Paris* (1832) Sir Walter Scott (1771–1832) gives a vivid description of its use during a sea-battle. This is based on an episode in the First Crusade, when a flotilla of the 'Latins' of western Europe, led by the warrior Tancred, advanced with an air of menace towards Constantinople – now Istanbul – and the Greek vessels rallied to defend the city. In the story two townsmen who had come out to see the fight have been warned by an experienced seaman to take cover.

'But what is the meaning of that red flag which the Greek Admiral has this instant hoisted?'

'Why, you see, neighbour,' answered Demetrius, 'yonder western heretic continues to advance without minding the

* By Colonel H. W. L. Hime in *The Origin of Artillery*.

various signs which our Admiral has made to him to desist, and now he hoists the bloody colours, as if a man should clench his fist and say, If you persevere in your uncivil intention, I will do so and so.'

'By St. Sophia,' said Lascaris, 'and that is giving him fair warning. But what is it the Imperial Admiral is about to do?'

'Run! run! friend Lascaris,' said Demetrius, 'or you will see more of that than perchance you have any curiosity for.'

Accordingly, to add the strength of example to precept, Demetrius himself girt up his loins, and retreated with the most edifying speed to the opposite side of the ridge, accompanied by the greater part of the crowd, who had tarried there to witness the contest which the newsmonger promised, and were determined to take his word for their own safety. The sound and sight which had alarmed Demetrius, was the discharge of a large portion of Greek fire, which perhaps may be best compared to one of those immense Congreve rockets of the present day, which takes on its shoulders a small grapnel or anchor, and proceeds groaning through the air, like a fiend over-burdened by the mandate of some inexorable magician, and of which the operation was so terrifying, that the crews of the vessels attacked by this strange weapon frequently forsook every means of defence, and ran themselves ashore. One of the principal ingredients of this dreadful fire was supposed to be naphtha, or the bitumen which is collected on the banks of the Dead Sea, and which, when in a state of ignition, could only be extinguished by a very singular mixture, and which it was not likely to come in contact with. It produced a thick smoke and loud explosion, and was capable, says Gibbon, of communicating its flames with equal vehemence in descent or lateral progress. In sieges, it was poured from the ramparts, or launched like our bombs, in red-hot balls of stone or iron, or it was darted in flax twisted round arrows and in javelins. It was considered as a state secret of the greatest importance; and for wellnigh four centuries it was unknown to the Mohammedans. But at length the composition was discovered by the Saracens, and used by them for repelling the crusaders, and overpowering the Greeks, upon whose side it had at one time been the most formidable implement of defence. Some exaggeration we must allow for a barbarous period; but there seems no doubt that the general description of the crusader Joinville should be admitted as correct: 'It came flying through the air,' says that good knight, 'like a winged dragon, about the thickness of a hogshead, with the report of thunder and the speed of lightning, and the darkness of the night was dispelled by this horrible illumination.'

Not only the bold Demetrius and his pupil Lascaris, but all the crowd whom they influenced, fled manfully when the commodore of the Greeks fired the first discharge; and as the other vessels in the squadron followed his example, the heavens were filled with the unusual and outrageous noise, while the smoke was so thick as to darken the very air. As the fugitives passed the crest of the hill, they saw the seaman, whom we formerly mentioned as a spectator, snugly reclining under cover of a dry ditch, where he managed so as to secure himself as far as possible from any accident. He could not, however, omit breaking his jest on the politicians.

'What, ho!' he cried, 'my good friends,' without raising himself above the counterscarp of his ditch, 'will you not remain upon your station long enough to finish that hopeful lecture upon battle by sea and land, which you had so happy an opportunity of commencing? Believe me, the noise is more alarming than hurtful; the fire is all pointed in a direction opposite to yours, and if one of those dragons which you see does happen to fly landward instead of seaward, it is but the mistake of some cabin-boy, who has used his linstock with more willingness than ability.'

Demetrius and Lascaris just heard enough of the naval hero's harangue, to acquaint them with the new danger with which they might be assailed by the possible misdirection of the weapons, and, rushing down towards the lists at the head of a crowd half-desperate with fear, they hastily propagated the appalling news, that the Latins were coming back from Asia with the purpose of landing in arms, pillaging, and burning the city.

The uproar, in the meantime, of this unexpected occurrence, was such as altogether to vindicate, in public opinion, the reported cause, however exaggerated. The thunder of the Greek fire came successively, one hard upon the other, and each, in its turn, spread a blot of black smoke upon the face of the landscape, which, thickened by so many successive clouds, seemed at last, like that raised by a sustained fire of modern artillery, to overshadow the whole horizon.

The small squadron of Tancred were completely hid from view in the surging volumes of darkness, which the breath of the weapons of the enemy had spread around him; and it seemed

by a red light, which began to show itself among the thickest of
the veil of darkness, that one of the flotilla at least had caught
fire. Yet the Latins resisted, with an obstinacy worthy of their
own courage and the fame of their celebrated leader. Some advantage they had, on account of their small size, and their low-
ness in the water, as well as the clouded state of the atmosphere,
which rendered them difficult marks for the fire of the Greeks.

To increase these advantages, Tancred, as well by boats as by
the kind of rude signals made use of at the period, dispersed
orders to his fleet, that each bark, disregarding the fate of the
others, should press forward individually, and that the men
from each should be put on shore wheresoever and howsoever
they could effect that manoeuvre. Tancred himself set a noble
example; he was on board a stout vessel, fenced in some degree
against the effect of the Greek fire by being in a great measure
covered with rawhides, which hides had also been recently
steeped in water. This vessel contained upwards of a hundred
valiant warriors, several of them of knightly order, who had all
night toiled at the humble labours of the oar, and now in the
morning applied their chivalrous hands to the arblast and to the
bow, which were in general accounted the weapons of persons of
a lower rank. Thus armed, and thus manned, Prince Tancred
bestowed upon his bark the full velocity which wind, and tide,
and oar, could enable her to obtain, and placing her in the situation to profit by them as much as his maritime skill could direct,
he drove with the speed of lightning among the vessels of Lemnos, plying on either side, bows, crossbows, javelins, and mili-
tary missiles of every kind, which the greater advantage that the
Greeks, trusting to their artificial fire, had omitted arming themselves with other weapons; so that when the valiant Crusader
bore down on them with so much fury, repaying the terrors of
their fire with a storm of bolts and arrows no less formidable,
they began to feel that their own advantage was much less than
they had supposed, and that, like most other dangers, the maritime fire of the Greeks, when undauntedly confronted, lost at
least one-half of its terrors. The Grecian sailors, too, when they
observed the vessels approach so near, filled with the steel-clad
Latins, began to shrink from a contest to be maintained hand to
hand with so terrible an enemy.

By degrees, smoke began to issue from the sides of the great
Grecian argosy, and the voice of Tancred announced to his
soldiers that the Grecian Admiral's vessel had taken fire, owing

to negligence in the management of the means of destruction she possessed and that all they had now to do was to maintain such a distance as to avoid sharing her fate. Sparkles and flashes of flame were next seen leaping from place to place on board of the great hulk, as if the element had had the sense and purpose of spreading wider with the consternation, and disabling the few who still paid attention to the commands of their Admiral, and endeavoured to extinguish the fire. The consciousness of the combustible nature of the freight, began to add despair to terror; from the boltsprit, the rigging, the yards, and sides, and every part of the vessel, the unfortunate crew were seen dropping themselves, to exchange for the most part a watery death for one by the more dreadful agency of fire. The crew of Tancred's bark, ceasing, by that generous prince's commands, to offer any additional annoyance to an enemy who was at once threated by the perils of the ocean and of conflagration, ran their vessel ashore in a smooth part of the bay, and jumping into the shallow sea, made the land without difficulty; many of their steeds being, by the exertions of the owners and the docility of the animals, brought ashore at the same time with their masters. Their commander lost no time in forming their serried ranks into a phalanx of lancers, few indeed at first, but perpetually increasing as ship after ship of the little flotilla ran ashore, or, having more deliberately moored their barks, landed their men, and joined their companions.

The cloud which had been raised by the conflict was now driven to leeward before the wind, and the strait exhibited only the relics of the combat. Here tossed upon the billows the scattered and broken remains of one or two of the Latin vessels which had been burnt at the commencement of the combat, though their crews, by the exertions of their comrades, had in general been saved. Lower down were seen the remaining five vessels of the Lemnos squadron, holding a disorderly and difficult retreat, with the purpose of gaining the harbour of Constantinople. In the place so late the scene of combat, lay moored the hulk of the Grecian Admiral, burnt to the water's edge, and still sending forth a black smoke from its scathed beams and planks. The flotilla of Tancred, busied in discharging its troops, lay irregularly scattered along the bay, the men making ashore as they could, and taking their course to join the standard of their leader. Various black substances floated on the surface of the water, nearer, or more distant to the shore; some proved to be the wreck of the vessels which had been destroyed, and others, more ominous still, the lifeless bodies of mariners who had fallen in the conflict.

The standard had been borne ashore by the prince's favourite page, Ernest of Apulia, so soon as the keel of Tancred's galley had grazed upon the sand. It was then pitched on the top of that elevated cape between Contantinople and the lists, where Lascaris, Demetrius, and other gossips, had held their station at the commencement of the engagement, but from which all had fled, between the mingled dread of the Greek fire and the missiles of the Latin crusaders.

THE VANISHED CIVILIZATION

PLATO

adapted from The *Timaeus* and *Critias*

One ancient tradition, too venerable and too evocative to be regarded as a wonder story, either has a factual basis or forms a classic example of science fiction. It has the same theme as many modern science fictional stories and has directly inspired others.* It has also given rise to much speculation: is the tradition based upon an actual occurrence or not?

It relates that long ago a mighty civilization flourished in what was then almost an unknown region, which lay beyond the Pillars of Hercules. Incredibly wealthy and powerful, it was at last destroyed by the gods because of its people's overweening pride.

The following summary is chiefly based on the two *Dialogues* of Plato, the *Timaeus* and the *Critias,* in which are described the splendour and the strength of Atlantis; one of these breaks off disappointingly just as the gods are about to discuss its punishment. This summary has been deliberately written in a somewhat archaic style which seems appropriate to the subject.

Immense as Atlantis traditionally was, it would not be so monstrous as this description might suggest, for 'Africa' means the region north of the Sahara, and 'Asia' means what is now called Asia Minor.

Was there ever an Atlantis, a gigantic highly civilized island out beyond the Pillars of Hercules? Or was this story based upon the vague tradition of some other bygone civilization which had vanished in less spectacular circumstances but just as completely? Or could it simply have been one of the parables with which Plato liked to drive his morals home, warning his contemporaries that if they were to value wealth and power rather than virtue they too would likewise perish?

A modern science fiction writer, had he been writing upon similar lines, would probably have made his warning more definite. He might explain that Atlantis had perished because its thinkers had been investigating atomic structure either

* Notably *The Lost Continent*, by C. J. Cutliffe Hyne.

through the side-effects of some ill-advised experiment or through its warriors having insisted, in spite of the protests of the philosophers, on exploding some sort of nuclear weapon.

This tradition, Plato explains, was expounded to the wise Greek statesman Solon by an ancient Egyptian priest.

IT is related in our records how in the distant past your city checked the advance of a mighty army which, setting out from a distant island in the Atlantic Ocean, was arrogantly approaching to attack all Europe and Asia as well. Now this island was very large – larger than Africa and Asia put together – and was situated opposite the Strait between the Pillars of Hercules.

This island of Atlantis was ruled by a family of kings, of great and wonderful power, who governed not only the whole island but many other islands and a part of the mainland; for they ruled over northern Africa as far as Egypt and over southern Europe as far as Italy.

Its government was founded by the god Poseidon, who divided the land among his ten sons. The eldest he made king of the whole island; and this was called Atlantis, and the ocean is still called the Atlantic, because Atlas was the name of the first king; and he made the king's brothers surbordinate princes, giving to each of them rule over many men and a wide expanse of country. And the descendants of Atlas multiplied, and their wealth and power was such that no monarch had ever known it before nor may ever do so again.

Not only did they import largely from abroad, but the island itself supplied almost everything needed for daily life: metals hard and soft and that metal which is now only a name but was then more than a name, the metal orichalcum, the most precious of all the metals except gold. And the fertile soil produced trees in abundance and the climate was so temperate that the fruits of the earth ripened twice a year, and there were many elephants and other animals both wild and tame.

The city on the hill in the centre of the island was three thousand feet in diameter and was wondrous to behold; for bridges had been built across the sea-channels which Poseidon had made, and a canal had been dug from the city to the sea, and a citadel had been built plated with tin and brass and the red orichalcum.

In the midst of the city was the royal palace and the great temple of Poseidon, which was secluded as holy and was bounded by a golden wall; it was covered with silver and pinnacles of gold towered above the roof of ivory. Within the temple was a golden statue of the god himself, so vast as to touch the roof and drawn by six winged horses, and around it were a hundred Nereids riding on dolphins, and outside the temple stood golden statues of all the princes of Atlantis with their wives.

And in the island were springs of hot and cold water, with baths and fountains and public gardens and groves. There were exercise grounds for men and for horses, and a vast race-course, and barracks and guardrooms and dockyards and harbours full of merchant vessels and ships of war.

The plain around the city was sheltered by the mountains and protected by a vast series of channels a hundred feet deep and six hundred feet broad, and in all more than three thousand miles long. Then ten kings who ruled the island held council together and vowed to assist one another in peace and war, and they had ten thousand chariots and a fleet of over a thousand ships.

For generation after generation the people of the island were obedient to the laws, and their kings governed wisely and righteously, setting no value on their wealth and caring only for virtue. But with time the divine part of their souls grew faint, and they were filled with lawless ambition and the yearning for power.

Then Zeus, king of the gods, realizing the evil condition into which this race had fallen, determined to punish them so that the chastisement might bring them to their senses. So assembling the gods he addressed them. . . .

So the armies of Atlantis banded together to seek to enslave Hellas and Egypt and the whole of the Mediterranean shores. And then it was, the Egyptian priest assured Solon, that the manhood of Athens had displayed its valour and might to all the world. At first as leader of the Hellenes and then standing alone when deserted by all the others, after facing the most deadly perils it defeated the invaders and erected a trophy, having preserved from slavery all who were not yet enslaved and generously freed the others.

But there followed appalling earthquakes and floods and in one terrible day and night the earth opened and engulfed all the warriors of Athens, while the great island of Atlantis vanished beneath the sea. And to this day the ocean at that spot is shallow and impassable, for it is choked by the muddy shoals which the island produced as it was engulfed.

INTERPLANETARY WARFARE

LUCIAN

from *A True Story*

Lucian (about A.D. 125 – 180) was a native of Samosata, a town in Asia Minor. He is said to have been apprenticed to his uncle, a sculptor, but to have abandoned art for literature and oratory, sometimes pleading in the law-courts and sometimes delivering entertaining lectures. A satirist almost by profession, avowedly 'serious only in his desire to please', he aimed his wit not only against the philosophy and religion of his time but also against its culture.

A True Story, he explains, is a 'more or less comical parody of the poets, historians, and philosophers of old, who have written much that smacks of miracle and fables'. He is scathing even about Homer, declaring that the wonders he describes were simply nonsensical yarns with which the wily Odysseus humbugged the illiterate barbarians who gave him hospitality.

For his own part, as he points out, he is at least truthful in confessing himself a liar who makes up his story as he goes along. Thus he demonstrates that if not actually the very earliest, he was at least one of the earliest, of writers of science fiction.*

Fantastic as his narrative is, it is said to have inspired such authors as Rabelais, Cyrano de Bergerac, Dean Swift, and Voltaire; not without reason, indeed, has Lucian been called 'the H. G. Wells of antiquity'.

Judged by modern standards, Lucian's bug-eyed monsters may seem unduly grotesque and monstrous, but that is an understandable fault in pioneer work, especially as he was deliberately being facetious. With their more absurd features modified, and with the most gigantic 'cut down to size', they would compare

* Roger Lancelyn Green's history of 'Space Flight in Fiction'. *Into Other Worlds*, mentions a lost 'fictitious travel book', entitled *Of the Wonderful Things beyond Thule*, which describes a voyage to the moon, but says that practically nothing is known of it or its author, Antonius Diogenes, not even the date when it was written.

with the BEMs of contemporary science fiction, possibly with
the Selenites and Martians of H. G. Wells.

Lucian resembles the modern science fiction writers in giving his creatures from outer space, however outlandish they are,
some of the social customs familiar to himself : to celebrate a victory by erecting a trophy, was, for example, a characteristic Greek
ceremony. He resembles them, too, in satirizing actual events, the
peace treaty he describes being a parody of that between Athens
and Sparta as recorded by Thucydides;* and his Cloud-Centaurs who turn up only after the battle is over, may be a jibe at
the heroic Spartans, traditionally slow in 'getting off the mark'.

The following extract from *A True Story* is taken, by permission of The Harvard University Press and Messrs. William
Heinemann, from the translation by A. M. Harmon in The Loeb
Classical Library. The narrative also includes such episodes as
an island inhabited by plant-women who inflict upon the unwary
a fate literally worse than death, those to yield to their blandish-
ments take root and become plant-men. It also challenges
comparison with Jonah by describing a sea-monster so vast that
it can swallow a whole vessel, complete with its crew. It ends with
a promise 'to be continued' – but that, as one of the Lucian's early
admirers commented disgustedly, was the biggest lie of all.

ONCE upon a time, setting out from the Pillars of Hercules and
heading for the western ocean with a fair wind, I went a-voyag-
ing. The motive and purpose of my journey lay in my intellectual
activity and desire for adventure, and in my wish to find out
what the end of the ocean was, and who the people were that
lived on the other side. On this account I put aboard a good store
of provisions, stowed water enough, enlisted in the venture fifty
of my acquaintances who were like-minded with myself, got
together also a great quantity of arms, shipped the best sailing-
master to be had at the big inducement, and put my boat – she
was a pinnace – in trim for a long and difficult voyage. Well, for
a day and a night we sailed before the wind without making very
much offing, as land was still dimly in sight; but at sunrise on
the second day the wind freshened, the sea rose, darkness came
on, and before we knew it we could no longer even get our canvas in. Committing ourselves to the gale and giving up, we drove
for seventy-nine days. On the eightieth day, however, the sun

* Roger Lancelyn Green, *ibid.*

came out suddenly and at no great distance we saw a high, wooded island ringed about with sounding surf, which, however, was not rough, as already the worst of the storm was abating.

.   .   .   .

About noon, when the island was no longer in sight, a whirlwind suddenly arose, spun the boat about, raised her into the air about three hundred furlongs and did not let her down into the sea again; but while she was hung up aloft a wind struck her sails and drove her ahead with bellying canvas. For seven days and seven nights we sailed the air, and on the eighth day we saw a great country in it, resembling an island, bright and round and shining with a great light. Running in there and anchoring, we went ashore, and on investigating found that the land was inhabited and cultivated. By day nothing was in sight from the place, but as night came on we began to see many other islands hard by, some larger, some smaller, and they were like fire in colour. We also saw another country below, with cities in it and rivers and seas and forests and mountains. This we inferred to be our own world.

We determined to go still farther inland, but we met what they call the Vulture Dragoons, and were arrested. These are men riding on large vultures and using the birds for horses. The vultures are large and for the most part have three heads: you can judge of their size from the fact that the mast of a large merchantman is not so long or so thick as the smallest of the quills they have. The Vulture Dragoons are commissioned to fly about the country and bring before the king any stranger they may find, so of course they arrested us and brought us before him. When he had looked us over and drawn his conclusions from our clothes, he said: 'Then you are Greeks, are you, strangers?' and when we assented, 'Well, how did you get here, with so much air to cross?' We told him all, and he began and told us about himself: that he too was a human being, Endymion by name, who had once been ravished from our country in his sleep, and on coming there had been made king of the land. He said that his country was the Moon that shines down on us. He urged us to take heart, however, and suspect no danger, for we should have everything that we required. 'And if I succeed,' he said, 'in the war which I am now making on the people of the Sun, you shall lead the happiest of lives with me.' We asked who the enemy were, and what the quarrel was about. 'Phaethon,' said he, 'the king of the inhabitants of the Sun – for it is inhabited, you know, as well as the Moon – has been at war with us for a long time now. It began in this way. Once upon a time I gathered together the poorest people in my kingdom and undertook to plant a colony on the Morning Star, which was empty and uninhabited. Phaethon out of jealousy thwarted the colonization, meeting us half-way at the head of his Ant Dragoons. At that time we were beaten, for we were not a match for them in strength, and we retreated: now, however, I desire to make war again and plant the colony. If you wish, then, you may take part with me in the expedition and I will give each of you one of my royal vultures and a complete outfit. We shall take the field tomorrow.' 'Very well,' said I, 'since you think it best.'

That night we stopped there as his guests, but at daybreak we arose and took our posts, for the scouts signalled that the enemy was near. The number of our army was a hundred thousand, apart from the porters, the engineers, the infantry and the foreign allies; of this total, eighty thousand were Vulture Dragoons and twenty thousand Grassplume-riders. The Grassplume is also a very large bird, which instead of plumage is all shaggy with grass and has wings very like lettuce-leaves. Next to these the Millet-shooters and the Garlic-fighters were posted. Endymion also had allies who came from the Great Bear – thirty thousand Flea-archers and fifty thousand Volplaneurs. The Flea-archers ride on great fleas, from which they get their name; the fleas are as large as twelve elephants. The Volplaneurs are infantry, to be sure, but they fly in the air without wings. As to the manner of their flight, they pull their long tunics up through their girdles, let the baggy folds fill with wind as if they were sails, and are carried along like boats. For the most part they serve as light infantry in battle. It was said, too, that the stars over Cappadocia would send seventy thousand Sparrowcorns and five thousand Crane Dragoons. I did not get a look at them, as they did not come, so I have not ventured to write about their characteristics, for the stories about them were wonderful and incredible.

These were the forces of Endymion. They all had the same equipment – helmets of beans (their beans are large and tough); scale-corselets of lupines (they sew together the skins of lupines to make the corselets, and in that country the skin of the lupine is unbreakable, like horn); shields and swords of the Greek pattern. When the time came, they took position thus; on the right wing, the Vulture Dragoons and the king, with the bravest about him (we were among them); on the left, the Grassplumes; in the centre, the allies, in whatever formation they liked. The infantry came to about sixty million, and was deployed as follows. Spiders in that country are numerous and large, all of them far larger than the Cyclades islands. They were commissioned by the king to span the air between the Moon and the Morning Star with a web, and as soon as they had finished and had made a plain, he deployed his infantry on it. Their leaders were Owlett son of Fairweather, and two others.

As to the enemy, on the left were the Ant Dragoons, with whom was Phaethon. They were very large beasts with wings, like the ants that we have, except in size: the largest one was two hundred feet long. They themselves fought, as well as their riders, and made especially good use of their feelers. They were said to number about fifty thousand. On their right were posted the Sky-mosquitoes, numbering also about fifty thousand, all archers riding on large mosquitoes. Next to them were the Sky-dancers, a sort of light infantry, formidable however, like all the rest, for they slung huge radishes at long range, and any man that they hit could not hold out a moment, but died, and his wound was malodorous. They were said to anoint their missiles with mallow poison. Besides them were posted the Stalk-mushrooms, heavy infantry employed at close quarters, ten thousand in number. They had the name Stalk-mushrooms because they used mushrooms for shields and stalks of asparagus for spears. Near them stood the Puppycorns, who were sent him by the inhabitants of the Dog-star, five thousand dogfaced men who fight on the back of winged acorns. It was said that there were tardy allies in Phaethon's case, too – the slingers whom he had summoned from the Milky Way, and the Cloud-centaurs. The latter, to be sure, arrived just after the battle was over (if only they had not!); but the slingers did not put in an appearance at all. On account of this, they say, Phaethon was furious with them and afterwards ravaged their country with fire.

This, then, was the array with which Phaethon came on. Joining battle when the flags had been flown and the donkeys on both sides had brayed (for they had donkeys for trumpeters), they fought. The left wing of the Sunites fled at once, without even receiving the charge of the Vulture Horse, and we pursued, cutting them down. But their right wing got the better of the left on our side, and the Sky-mosquitoes advanced in pursuit right up to the infantry. Then, when the infantry came to the rescue, they broke and fled, especially as they saw that the forces on their left had been defeated. It was a glorious victory, in which many were taken alive and many were slain; so much blood flowed on the clouds that they were dyed and looked red, as they do in our country when the sun is setting, and so much also dripped down on the earth that I wonder whether something of the sort did not take place in the sky long ago, when Homer supposed that Zeus had sent a rain of blood on account of the death of Sarpedon.

When we had returned from the pursuit we set up two trophies, one on the spider-webs for the infantry battle and the other, for the sky battle, on the clouds. We were just doing this when the scouts reported that the Cloud-centaurs, who should have come to Phaethon's aid before the battle, were advancing on us. Before we knew it, they were coming on in plain sight, a most unparalleled spectacle, being a combination of winged horses and men. In size the men were as large as the Colossus of Rhodes from the waist up, and the horses were as large as a great merchantman. Their number, however, I leave unrecorded for fear that someone may think it incredible, it was so great. Their leader was the Archer from the Zodiac. When they saw that their friends had been defeated, they sent word to Phaethon to advance again, and then, on their own account, in regular formation fell on the disordered Moonites, who had broken ranks and scattered to pursue and to plunder. They put them all to flight, pursued the king himself to the city and killed most of his birds; they plucked up the trophies and overran the whole plain woven by the spiders, and they captured me with two of my comrades. By this time Phaethon too was present, and other trophies were being set up by his side.

As for us, we were taken off to the Sun that day, our hands tied behind our backs with a section of spider-web. The enemy decided not to lay siege to the city, but on their way back they built a wall through the air, so that the rays of the Sun should no longer reach the Moon. The wall was double, made of cloud, so that a genuine eclipse of the Moon took place, and she was completely enshrouded in unbroken night. Hard pressed by this, Endymion sent and begged them to pull down the construction and not let them lead their lives in darkness. He promised to pay tribute, to be an ally and not to make war again, and volunteered to give hostages for all this. Phaethon and his people held two assemblies; on the first day they did not lay aside a particle of their anger, but on the second day they softened, and the peace was made on these terms:

On the following conditions the Sunites and their allies make peace with the Moonites and their allies to wit:

that the Sunites tear down the dividing-wall and do not invade the Moon again, and that they make over the prisoners of war, each at a set ransom;

that the Moonites permit the stars to be autonomous, and do not make war on the Sunites;

that each country aid the other if it be attacked;

that in yearly tribute the King of the Moonites pay the King of the Sunites ten thousand gallons of dew, and that he give ten thousand of his people as hostages;

that the colony on the Morning Star be planted in common, and that anyone else who so desires may take part in it;

that the treaty be inscribed on a slab of electrum and set up in mid-air, on the common confines.

Attested under hand and seal.

(For the Sunites)	(For the Moonites)
Firebrace	Darkling
Parcher	Moony
Burns	Allbright

On those terms peace was made, and then the wall was torn down at once and we prisoners were restored. When we reached the Moon we were met and tearfully welcomed by our comrades and by Endymion himself. He wanted me to stay with him and join the colony, promising to give me his own son in marriage – there are no women in their country. But I was not to be persuaded; I asked him to let me go down to the sea. When he perceived that he could not prevail on me, he let us go after entertaining us for seven days.

.   .   .   .   .   .

To go back to my story, we embraced the king and his friends, went aboard, and put off. Endymion even gave me presents – two of the glass tunics, five of bronze, and a suit of lupine armour – but I left them all behind in the whale. He also sent a thousand Vulture Dragoons with us to escort us for sixty miles. On our way we passed many countries and put in at the Morning Star, which was just being colonized. He landed there and procured water. Going aboard and making for the Zodiac, we passed the Sun to port, hugging the shore. We did not land, though many of my comrades wanted to; for the wind was unfavourable. But we saw that the country was green and fertile and well watered, and full of untold good things. On seeing us, the Cloud-centaurs, who had entered the service of Phaethon, flew up to the ship and then went away again when they found out that the treaty protected us. The Vulture Dragoons had already left us.

Sailing the next night and day we reached the city called Lamptown towards evening, already being on our downward way. This city lies in the air midway between the Pleiades and the Hyades, though much lower than the Zodiac. On landing, we did not find any men at all, but a lot of lamps running about and loitering in the public square and at the harbour. Some of them were small and poor, so to speak: a few, being great and powerful, were very splendid and conspicuous. Each of them has his own house, or sconce, they have names like men, and we heard them talking. They offered us no harm, but invited us to be their guests. We were afraid, however, and none of us ventured to eat a mouthful or close an eye. They have a public building in the centre of the city, where their magistrate sits all night and calls each of them by name, and whoever does not answer is sentenced to death for deserting. They are executed by being put out. We were at court, saw what went on, and heard the lamps defend themselves and tell why they came late. There I recognized our own lamp: I spoke to him and inquired how things were at home, and he told me all about them.

That night we stopped there, but on the next day we set sail and continued our voyage. By this time we were near the clouds. There we saw the city of Cloudcuckootown, and wondered at it, but did not visit it, as the wind did not permit The king, however, was said to be Crow Dawson. It made me think of Aristophanes the poet, a wise and truthful man whose writings are distrusted without reason. On the next day but one, the ocean was already in plain sight, but no land anywhere except the countries in the air, and they began to appear fiery and bright. Towards noon on the fourth day the wind fell gently and gave out, and we were set down on the sea. When we touched the water we were marvellously pleased and happy, made as merry as we could in every way, and went over the side for a swim, for by good luck it was calm and the sea was smooth.

THE MOON-VOYAGE

JOHANNES KEPLER

adapted from *Somnium*

Lucian, author of *A True Story*, wrote another space-travel narrative, *Icaromenippus*, whose hero soared to the moon by attaching to one of his shoulders an eagle's wing and to the other a vulture's. Annoyed at his presumption, however, the gods stripped him of his plumage and restored him, gently but firmly, to earth.

Apart from magical wonder stories, there was little scope for science fiction during the Dark Ages, but by the seventeenth century the recent advances in astronomy had revived an interest in space travel. Galileo's telescope had confirmed an ancient belief that there were mountains and valleys on the moon,* and had incorrectly suggested that its dark patches were seas. The natural deduction – though Galileo himself thought it improbable – was that the moon might be inhabited.

It was only to be expected, then, that a number of moon-travel stories should be written, most of them purely fanciful: there were even stage-plays and operas based on the same theme, at least one by an established writer.† These stories tended to become either 'Utopian' or satirical, contrasting the moon's inhabitants with those of earth, usually to the latter's disadvantage. The methods of space travel mentioned in the story were mostly about as probable, and were intended as seriously, as the bird-wings or the gale in Lucian's two stories.

In Bishop Godwin's *The Man in the Moon* (1638) the involuntary astronaut is towed to his destination by a team of wild geese. Cyrano de Bergerac, in his *Comical Story of the States and Empires of the Moon* (1657), asserts that he was sucked aloft first by the evaporation of dew, and then by a 'flying chariot' aided by the attachment of some 'booster' rockets (the least preposterous of these suggestions); and, when these had burned out,

---

* Plutarch, *Of the Face in the Orb of the Moon*.
† Aphra Behn, *The Emperor of the Moon: A Farce*.

as the animal marrow with which he had anointed his bruises was 'sucked up' by the waning moon. De Foe's satire *The Consolidator* (1705) suggests that its author had an inkling of the internal-combustion engine when he describes immense wings worked by springs and wheels and actuated by 'an ambient flame, which fed on a certain spirit deposited in a proper quality to last out the voyage'.

In contrast with these fantasies, however, two seventeenth-century thinkers were considering quite seriously the probability of there being living creatures upon the moon. Possibly the first practical discussion of the problems of space travel – practical, of course, in the light of the knowledge of the time – is Bishop Wilkins' *The Discovery of a World in the Moone* (1638). While maintaining that the moon is inhabited, the Bishop, a founder-member of the Royal Society, refused to speculate about the nature of its inhabitants and went on to suggest possible methods of reaching them. He though it 'not altogether improbable' that some inventor might succeed in soaring about twenty miles into the air, and that beyond that height, 'without the Sphere of the Earth's Magnetical Vigor' gravitation might cease, so that journeying onwards to the moon should present no difficulty.

There would of course be the problems of breathing and eating during the journey, and he gives only a tentative glance at these. While thinking it 'not perhaps impossible' that flight be accomplished, after the style of Lucian's *Icaromenippus,* by the use of artificial wings, or on the back of what *The Arabian Nights* calls a roc, he suggests, something much more likely:

'Yet I do seriously, and upon good Grounds, affirm it possible to make a Flying Chariot, in which a man may sit, and give such a motion unto it, as shall convey him through the Air. And this perhaps might be made large enough to carry divers Men at the same time, together with Food for their *Viaticum,* and Commodities for Traffique.

'So that notwithstanding all these seeming impossibilities, 'tis likely enough, that there may be means invented of Journeying to the Moone. And how happy shall they be that are first successful in this attempt!'

Bishop Wilkins, a man of wide interests, may have read what is probably the first example of what might be called realistic science fiction, meant to convey astronomical information in story form, imaginative but based on contemporary knowledge. The author of *Somnium* (1634), Johannes Kepler, was himself an astronomer, mathematical, assistant to the great astronomer Tycho Brahe, whose observatory at Hven, near Elsinore, was called Uraniborg, 'the castle of the heavens'; his famous Three Laws of Planetary Motion paved the way for the work of Newton.

A mystic as well as a scientist, Kepler had a firm belief in the supernatural – understandably enough, for his own mother had narrowly escaped condemnation as a witch. He could therefore legitimately invoke supernatural assistance to convey his young space traveller to the moon.

Somnium has apparently never been translated into English, but it has been ably summarized by Patrick Moore in his book *Science and Fiction*, from which, with his permission and that of his publishers, George G. Harrap & Co. Ltd., the following extract has been quoted.

The hero of the *Somnium* is a young Icelander, Duracotus, whose parents were fisher-folk. Duracotus had no clear recollection of his father, who had died at the advanced age of 150 while the boy was still young, but his mother, Fiolxhilda, was very much to be reckoned with. Fiolxhilda was a 'wise woman', who earned her living by providing sailors with bags of magical herbs. One day Duracotus tampered with one of the bags, and destroyed it. His mother was so angry that she handed him over to the sailor who had been promised the charm, and when the ship left Iceland Duracotus left with it as an unwilling member of the crew.

The ship sailed across the Atlantic, until at last it reached the coast of Denmark. Duracotus had been of little help as a sea-man, and the captain had no further use for him, so he decided to use him solely as a messenger-boy. In Denmark lived the famous astronomer Tycho Brahe, and Duracotus was dispatched to take Tycho some letters which the captain wished to be delivered.

Tycho received the boy kindly, and saw that he was a youth of real talent. He even offered to instruct him in the wonders of astronomy, and Duracotus was only too ready to learn; he spent five years on Hven, and when at last he left for home he knew almost as much about the heavens as Tycho himself. Yet in spite of everything he could not forget his mother, and when he arrived back in Iceland he was overjoyed to find her alive and well.

Duracotus soon found that there was little he could teach Fiolxhilda about astronomy. He himself had been instructed by a great scientist, but Tycho, brilliant though he was, was a man and nothing more. Fiolxhilda's teacher was a demon, who lived not in Scandinavia, but in 'Levania', the Moon.

Fiolxhilda was cautious, but at last she made up her mind to reveal some of her secrets. Both Levania and 'Volva', the Earth, contain demons; but in the ordinary way no demons can cross from one world to the other, because they hate light, and the rays of the Sun are too brilliant. Occasionally, however, the shadow of the Earth falls on to the Moon, and for an hour or two there is a bridge of darkness across which the demons can pass at will.

The Moon is not self-luminous, and shines only because it reflects the light of the Sun. Like any other solid and nonradiating body, the Earth casts a shadow in space, so that when the Sun, Earth, and Moon move into a straight line, with the Earth in the middle, this shadow cuts the sunlight off from the Moon's surface. This is what is known as a lunar eclipse, and if the Moon passes wholly into the shadow the eclipse is said to be total. Generally the Moon does not vanish completely, since the Earth's blanket of air bends some of the sun-rays on to the lunar disk, but instead of shining with its normal brilliance, the Moon turns a dim, sometimes coppery colour. Eclipses do not happen every month, owing to the tilt of the Moon's orbit, but on an average there are at least three per year.

Duracotus wanted to make the journey for himself. This could be managed, since the demons were obliging enough to take human tourists now and then, and at last all was ready. By means of her charms Fiolxhilda summoned the demons of Levania, and then 'withdrawing from me into the nearest crossroads', as Duracotus wrote, 'then returned; and commanding silence with the palm of her right hand outstretched, sat down near me. Scarcely had we covered our heads with a cloth, as is the custom, then behold, there came the sound of a voice ...'

So far the story of the *Somnium* has been pure fantasy, but from now on we start to find a mixture of true sixteenth-century silence. It is stressed that the journey along the bridge of shadow must always be far from comfortable, as human beings are

affected by coldness and by the lack of air. This latter point is
significant, and here at least Kepler's story is more plausible than
Lucian's.

The old philosophers had thought the air to extend to the far-
thest reaches of the universe, but Kepler knew better. Centuries
before, the Arab astronomers had calculated that the atmosphere
can extend upward for not more than a thousand miles. This
was a remarkably good guess; nowadays it is known that air resistance becomes very slight above only 120 miles or so, while
studies of the electrical phenomena known as aurorae polaris,
or Polar Lights, have shown that even at altitudes of 700 to 800
miles there is a trace of air left. On the other hand, it is a quarter
of a million miles to the Moon, and Kepler reasoned that most of
the journey must be done in vacuum. Duracotus was accordingly
given an anaethetic, or 'dozing draught', to ease the discomfort;
he was also given sponges, which were moistened and held to
the nostrils. Short of equipping his hero with a space-suit, Kepler
could hardly have done any better, and this is the first indication that the *Somnium* is meant to be something rather more
than a mere story.

Even more significant is the fact that Kepler did not over-
look the effect of what we now call gravity. He had discovered
how the planets move; he had not discovered why they move
in such a way, but he was certainly on the right track. He describes how the demons' part was done when they had pulled
Duracotus up to the point where the Moon's force balances that
of the Earth. After this point had been reached they simply let
go, and allowed their passenger to fall towards the Moon on
his own. We have, in fact, the first indication of the 'neutral
point' between the two bodies, later to be used – or, rather, mis-
used – by no less a writer than Jules Verne.

Moreover, Duracotus relates that as soon as he arrived at the
neutral point his limbs curled up like those of a spider. 'When
the attractions of the Moon and of the Earth equalize each other,
it is as though neither of them exerted any attraction. Then the
body itself, being the whole, attracts its minor parts, its limbs,
because the body is the whole.' Nothing could be clearer. Kepler
is describing gravity. He did not understand it, of course, and
even refers to it as 'magnetic influence', but he is describing
it none the less.

So much for the voyage itself. Kepler had to use supernatural
means simply because he knew of no other, but as soon as

Duracotus reaches the Moon the story becomes purely scientific. At that time it was still believed that the Moon was a smaller edition of the Earth, with air, oceans, and inhabitants. It was only a few years since Galileo had turned his first crude telescope to the heavens and had constructed the first lunar map, so Kepler had no means of guessing that the real Moon is airless, waterless, and lifeless. His description of our satellite is in accord with the facts as he knew them.

From the astronomer's point of view, the Moon behaves in an infuriating way inasmuch as it keeps one hemisphere turned permanently away from the Earth. It revolves round us in $27\frac{1}{3}$ days, but it also spins on its axis in $27\frac{1}{3}$ days, so that there is a part of the Moon which we can never see. (The best way to show what is meant is to walk round a chair, keeping your face towards the chair-seat all the time. By the time you have completed one revolution you will have turned once on your axis; the back of your head, representing the back of the Moon, will not have been turned towards the chair at all.) This means that to an observer standing on the lunar surface of the Earth will appear to remain almost stationary in the sky, while from the averted hemisphere the Earth can never be seen.

Kepler knew this, and Duracotus related how Levania is divided into two zones, Subvolva and Privolva. From Subvolva the 'Volva', or Earth, is always visible; from Privolva, never. In general, he finds that Levania is a world of extremes, with violent changes of climate, towering mountains, and deep valleys.

'The hollows of the Moon first seen by Galileo are portions below the general level, like our oceans, but their appearance makes me judge that they are swampy for the greater part. It is there that the Endymionides find the sites for the fortified cities which protect them against the swampiness as well as against the heat of the Sun, possibly also against the enemies.'

Lucian's King of the Moon had been Endymion; now we find Kepler referring to the lunar inhabitants as Endymionides, but there the resemblance ends. The Moon-folk of the *Somnium* are not human either in mind or in body. Some are of a serpent-like form, while others have fins to propel them through the water, and still others crawl along the ground. Most are covered with fur. When a Moon creature is unwise enough to allow itself to be caught in the open near midday its outer fur is singed by the intense heat, so that the creature drops as though dead. At nightfall it revives, and the singed parts of its fur simply fall away.

Government and civilization in the terrestrial sense cannot exist on Levania, mainly because of the brief life-span of its inhabitants. In Subvolva, particularly, the creatures and plants are of monstrous size, but live for only a few lunar days. This is more or less what would be expected upon a moist, fiercely hot world, as Kepler believed the daytime Subvolva to be.

There is some truth in Duracotus' word-picture. As the Moon rotates so slowly, a 'day' there is as long as a fortnight on Earth, and the equatorial temperature can attain +216 degrees Fahrenheit, above that of boiling water. At midnight, however, this temperature drops to —250 degrees Fahrenheit, so that air would freeze. Moreover, the lunar peaks are higher than ours, both relatively and absolutely; recent measures of the lunar Leibnitz Mountains show that they attain a height of 30,000 feet, which is greater than that of Everest. The depths of the cracks or clefts are still rather uncertain, but must be considerable, so that the Moon is indeed a world of extremes. What Kepler did not know, and could not know, is that it is virtually airless and completely without liquid, so that his plants and Endymionides cannot exist outside the pages of a book.

Yet Kepler cheats us in the end. At the very beginning of his tale he tells how he himself lay down one night after a period of watching the skies, and drifted presently into a doze. At the very last we learn that the whole story has been a dream; that Duracotus, Fiolxhilda, and Endymionides, and the Levanian demons were part of it, and that he awoke to find 'his head covered with a cushion, and his body tangled in a rug'. We see now why Kepler called his book the *Somnium*.

The main difference between the stories of Lucian and Kepler is that the Greek satirist was writing in light-hearted vein, and was not in the least concerned whether his tale was factually correct or not, while Kepler could not break away from science. The *Somnium* is of distinct value. More clearly than in any other of his works, it shows that Kepler had a good idea of Newtonian gravitation, even though he could not put it into mathematical form. It shows, too that he knew that the Earth's atmosphere cannot extend all the way to the Moon.

UTOPIAN SCIENCE FICTION

FRANCIS BACON

from *The New Atlantis*

The tradition of Ancient Atlantis stimulated not only science fiction but the attempt to imagine those ideal commonwealths often called 'Utopias'.* Many of them, like their prototype, Plato's *Republic,* are chiefly concerned with social organization and religious background, but even one of the most idealistic, Sir Thomas More's *Utopia,* includes the mention of a technical development that must have seemed to most of his contemporaries like something out of science fiction, the hatching of chickens in incubators!

Francis Bacon (1561–1626), who was anxious for the advancement of human knowledge, wrote several works devoted to this subject. In *The New Atlantis* (1626) he seeks to describe a land in which, thanks to the co-operation of what would nowadays be called the scientists, the advancement has been achieved: instead of working in secrecy, like the alchemists of old, they pool their results, using a subdivision of labour somewhat suggestive of the methods of certain modern research institutes.

This refutes the idea that science fiction in general, and 'utopianization' in particular, is mere idle day-dreaming, for Bacon's 'House of Salomon' helped to bring about the formation of what was at first called 'The Invisible College' and is now the Royal Society.

The matter-of-fact style of the narrative's opening, suggesting the records of a real voyage, became almost standardized both for tales of adventure, like *Robinson Crusoe,* and for the early examples of science fiction, like *Gulliver's Travels*. It conveys verisimilitude, so that the reader, sometimes further reassured by its deeply religious tone, is prepared to accept the marvels that follow.

Needless to say, Bacon gives due attention both to the social

* Coined from the Greek by Sir Thomas More, the word 'Utopia' may be regarded as meaning either 'no place' or 'beautiful place'!

organization of his ideal commonwealth and to its religious background, which is a tolerant non-sectarian Christianity; he even
explains how the New Atlantis was miraculously evangelized.
Certain passages not quoted here show, however, that, like most
other Utopographers, his imagination could soar only when it
dealt with scientific knowledge and technics. He who could
foresee such marvels as the telephone and the submarine, as well
as 'some degrees of flying in the air', could not envisage the possibility of mixed bathing or the technical invention of a bathing
costume.

Such passages show, too, that when it came into family rela-
tionships he could not rise above the prejudices of his time. He
describes in rather wearisome detail an elaborate and costly ceremony held expressly to honour at public expense any father
who has presented the state with a very large family. And the
mother, who might reasonably be regarded as deserving of at
least some of the credit for this achievement? She is graciously
allowed to look on at the proceedings through a richly decorated
window – so long as she keeps out of sight.

WE sailed from Peru, where we had continued by the space
of one whole year, for China and Japan, by the South Sea, taking with us victuals for twelve months; and had good winds
from the east, though soft and weak, for five months' space and
more. But then the wind came about, and settled in the west for
many days, so as we could make little or no way, and were sometimes in purpose to turn back. But then again there arose strong
and great winds from the south, with a point east; which carried us up, for all that we could do, towards the north: by which
time our victuals failed us, though we had made good spare of
them. So that finding ourselves, in the midst of the greatest
wilderness of waters in the world, without victual, we gave ourselves for lost men, and prepared for death. Yet we did lift up
our hearts and voices to God above, who showeth His wonders
in the deep; beseeching Him of his mercy, that as in the beginning, He discovered the face of the deep, and brought forth dry
land, so He would now discover land to us, that we might not
perish. And it came to pass, that the next day about evening we
saw within a kenning before us, towards the north, as it were
thick clouds, which did put us in some hope of land: know-
ing how that part of the South Sea was utterly unknown: and

might have islands or continents, that hitherto were not come to light. Wherefore we bent our course thither, where we saw the appearance of land, all that night: and in the dawning of next day, we might plainly discern that it was a land flat to our sight, and full of boscage, which made it show the more dark. And after an hour and a half's sailing, we entered into a good haven, being the port of a fair city. Not great indeed, but well built, and that gave a pleasant view from the sea. And we thinking every minute long till we were on land, came close to the shore and offered to land. But straightways we saw divers of the people, with bastons in their hands, as it were forbidding us to land: yet without any cries or fierceness, but only as warning us off, by signs that they made. Whereupon, being not a little discomfited, we were advising with ourselves that we should do. During which time there made forth to us a small boat, with about eight persons in it, whereof one of them had in his hand a tipstaff of a yellow cane, tipped at both ends with blue, who made aboard our ship, without any show of distrust at all. And when he saw one of our number present himself somewhat afore the rest, he drew forth a little scroll of parchment (somewhat yellower than our parchment, and shining like the leaves of writing tables, but otherwise soft and flexible), and delivered it to our foremost man. In which scroll were written in ancient Hebrew, and in ancient Greek, and in good Latin of the school, and in Spanish these words: 'Land ye not, none of you, and provide to be gone from this coast within sixteen days, except you have further time given you; meanwhile, if you want fresh water, or victual, or help for your sick, or that your ship needeth repair, write down your wants, and you shall have that which belongeth to mercy.' This scroll was signed with a stamp of cherubim's wings, not spread, but hanging downwards; and by them a cross. This being delivered, the officer returned, and left only a servant with us to receive our answer. Consulting her upon amongst ourselves, we were much perplexed. The denial of landing, and hasty warning us away, troubled us much: on the other side, to find that the people had languages, and were so full of humanity, did comfort us not a little. And above all, the sign of the cross to that instrument, was to us a great rejoicing and as it were a certain presage of good. Our answer was in the Spanish tongue, 'That for our ship, it was well; for we had rather met with calms and contrary winds, than any tempests. For our sick, they were many, and in very ill case; so that if they were not permitted to land, they ran in danger of their lives.' Our other wants we set down in particular, adding, 'That we had some little store of merchandise, which if it pleased them to deal for, it might supply our wants, without being chargeable unto them.' We offered some reward in pistolets unto the servant, and a piece of crimson velvet to be presented to the officer; but the servant took them not, nor would scarce look upon them; and so left us, and went back in another little boat which was sent for him.

[After being allowed out of quarantine, the whole ship's company are made free of the New Atlantis, and are even allowed to kiss the end of the 'tippet' (some sort of cape or robe) of a very high official, the 'father of Salomon's House'. He especially honours the narrator by describing that institution, the forerunner of our own Department of Scientific and Industrial Research.]

'God bless thee, my son; I will give thee the greatest jewel I have. For I will impart unto thee, for the love of God and men, a relation of the true state of Salomon's House, I will keep this order. First, I will set forth unto you the end of our foundation. Secondly, the preparations and instruments we have for our works. Thirdly, the several employments and functions whereto our fellows are assigned. And fourthly, the ordinances and rites which we observe.

'The end of our foundation is the knowledge of causes, and secret motions of things; and the enlarging of the bounds of human empire, to the effecting of all things possible.

'The preparations and instruments are these. We have large and deep caves of several depths; the deepest are sunk 600 fathoms; and some of them are digged and made under great hills and mountains; so that if you reckon together the depth of the hill, and the depth of the cave, they are, some of them, above three miles deep. For we find that the depth of an hill, and the depth of a cave from the flat, is the same thing; both remote alike from the sun and heaven's beams, and from the open air. These caves we call the lower region. And we use them for all coagulations, indurations, refrigerations, and conservations of bodies. We use them likewise for the imitation of natural mines and the producing also of new artificial metals, by compositions and materials which we use and lay there for many years. We use them also sometimes (which may seem strange) for curing of some diseases, and for prolongation of life, in some hermits that choose to live there, well accommodated of all things necessary, and indeed live very long; by whom also we learn many things.

'We have burials in several earths, where we put divers cements, as the Chinese do their porcelain. But we have them in greater variety, and some of them more fine. We also have great variety of composts and soils, for the making of the earth fruitful.

'We have high towers, the highest about half a mile in height, and some of them likewise set upon high mountains, so that the vantage of the hill with the tower, is in the highest of them three miles at least. And these places we call the upper region, account the air between the high places and the low, as a middle region. We use these towers, according to their several heights and situations, for insulation, refrigeration, conservation, and for the view of divers meteors – as winds, rain, snow, hail; and some of the fiery meteors also. And upon them, in some places, are dwellings of hermits, whom we visit sometimes, and instruct what to observe.

'We have great lakes, both salt and fresh, whereof we have use for the fish and fowl. We use them also for the burials of some natural bodies, for we find a difference in things buried in earth, or in air below the earth, and things buried in water. We have also pools, of which some do strain fresh water out of salt, and others by art do turn fresh water into salt. We have also some rocks in the midst of the sea, and some bays upon the shore for some works, wherein is required the air and vapour of the sea. We have likewise violent streams and cataracts, which serve us for many motions; and likewise engines for multiplying and enforcing of winds to set also on divers motions.

'We have also a number of artificial wells and fountains, made in imitation of the natural sources and baths, as tincted upon vitriol, sulphur, steel, brass, lead, nitre, and other minerals; and again, we have little wells for infusions of many things, where the waters take the virtue quicker and better than in vessels or basins. And amongst them we have a water, which we call water of Paradise, being by that we do it made very sovereign for health and prolongation of life.

'We have also great and spacious houses, where we imitate and demonstrate meteors – as snow, hail, rain, some artificial rains of bodies, and not of water, thunders, lightnings; also generation of bodies of air – as frogs, flies, and divers others.

'We have also certain chambers, which we call chambers of health, where we qualify the air as we think good and proper for the cure of divers diseases, and preservation of health.

'We have also fair and large baths, of several mixtures, for the cure of diseases, and the restoring of man's body from arefaction; and others for the confirming of it in strength of sinews, vital parts, and the very juice and substance of the body.

'We have also large and various orchards and gardens, wherein we do not so much respect beauty as variety of ground and soil, proper for divers trees and herbs, and some very spacious, where trees and berries are set, whereof we make divers kinds of drinks, besides the vineyards. In these we practise likewise all conclusions of grafting, and inoculating, as well of wild-trees as fruit-trees, which produceth many effects. And we make by art, in the same orchards and gardens, trees and flowers, to come earlier or later than their seasons, and to come up and bear more speedily than by their natural course they do. We make them also by art greater much than their nature; and their fruit greater and sweeter, and of differing taste, smell, colour, and figure, from their nature. And many of them we so order, as that they become of medicinal use.

'We have also means to make divers plants rise by mixtures of earths without seeds, and likewise to make divers new plants, differing from the vulgar, and to make one tree or plant turn into another.

'We have also parks, and enclosures of all sorts, of beasts and birds; which we use not only for view or rareness, but likewise for dissections and trials, that thereby may take light what may be wrought upon the body of man. Wherein we find many strange effects: as continuing life in them, though divers parts, which you account vital, be perished and taken forth; resuscitating of some that seem dead in appearance, and the like. We try also all poisons, and other medicines upon them, as well of chirurgery as physic. By art likewise we make them greater or smaller than their kind is, and contrariwise dwarf them and stay their growth; we make them more fruitful and bearing than their kind is, and contrariwise barren and not generative. Also we make them differ in colour, shape, activity, many ways. We find means to make commixtures and copulations of divers kinds, which have produced many new kinds, and them not barren, as the general opinion is. We make a number of kinds of serpents, worms, flies, fishes of putrefaction, whereof some are advanced (in effect) to be perfect creatures, like beasts or birds, and have sexes, and do propagate. Neither do we this by chance, but we know beforehand of what matter and commixture, what kind of those creatures will arise.

'We have also particular polls where we make trials upon fishes, as we have said before of beasts and birds.

'We have also places for breed and generation of those kinds of worms and flies which are of special use; such as are with you your silkworms and bees.

'I will not hold you long with recounting of our brew-houses, bake-houses, and kitchens, where are made divers drinks, breads, and meats, rare and of special effects. Wines we have of grapes, and drinks of other juice, of fruits, of grains, and of roots, and of mixtures with honey, sugar, manna, and fruits dried and decocted; also of the tears or wounding of trees, and of the pulp of canes. And these drinks are of several ages, some to the age or last of forty years. We have drinks also brewed with several herbs and roots, and spices; yea, with several fleshes, and white-meats; whereof some of the drinks are such as they are in effect meat and drink both, so that divers, especially in age, do desire to live with them with little or no meat or bread. And above all we strive to have drinks of extreme thin parts, to insinuate into the body, and yet without all biting, sharpness, or fretting; insomuch as some of them put upon the back of your hand, will with a little stay pass through to the palm, and yet taste mild to the mouth. We have also waters, which we ripen in that fashion, as they become nourishing, so that they are indeed excellent drinks, and many will use no other. Bread we have of several grains, roots, and kernels; yes, and some of flesh, and fish, dried; with divers kinds of leavings and seasonings; so that some do extremely move appetites, some do nourish so, as divers do live of them, without any other meat, who live very long. So for meats, we have some of them so beaten, and made tender, and mortified, yet without all corrupting, as a weak heat of the stomach will turn into good chilus, as well as a strong heat would meat otherwise prepared. We have some meats also and bread, and drinks, which taken by men, enable them to fast long after; and some other, that used make the very flesh of men's bodies sensibly more hard and tough, and their strength far greater than otherwise it would be.

'We have dispensatories or shops of medicines; wherein you may easily think, if we have such variety of plants, and living creatures, more than you have in Europe (for we know what you have), the simples, drugs, and ingredients of medicines, must likewise be in so much the greater variety. We have them likewise of divers ages, and long fermentations. And for their preparations, we have not only all manner of exquisite distillations, and separations, and especially by gentle heats, and percolations through divers strainers, yea, and substances; but also exact forms of composition, whereby they incorporate almost as they were natural simples.

'We have also divers mechanical arts, which you have not; and stuffs made by them, as papers, linen, silks, tissues, dainty works of feathers of wonderful lustre, excellent dyes, and many others, and shops likewise as well for such as are not brought into vulgar use amongst us, as for those that are. For you must know, that of the things before recited, many of them are grown into use throughout the kingdom, but yet, if they did flow from our invention, we have of them also for patterns and principals.

'We have also furnaces of great diversities, and that keep great diversity of hearts; fierce and quick, strong and constant, soft and mild, blown, quiet, dry, moist, and the like. But above all we have heats, in imitation of the sun's heavenly bodies' heats, that pass divers inequalities, and as it were orbs, progresses, and returns whereby we produce admirable effects. Besides, we have heats of dungs, and of bellies and maws of living creatures and of their bloods and bodies, and of hays and herbs laid up moist, of lime unquenched, and such like. Instruments also which generate heat only by motion. And farther, places for strong insulations; and again, places under the earth, which by nature or art yield heat. These divers heats we use, as the nature of the operation which we intend requireth.

'We have also perspective-houses, where we make demonstrations of all lights and radiation, and of all colours; and out of things uncoloured and transparent, we can represent unto you all several colours, not in rainbows, as it is in gems and prisms, but of themselves single. We represent also all multiplications of light, which we carry to great distance, and make so sharp, as to discern small points and lines. Also all colourations of light; all delusions and deceits of the sight, in figures, magnitudes, motions, colours; all demonstrations of shadows. We find also divers means, yet unknown to you, of producing of light, originally from divers bodies. We procure means of seeing objects afar off, as in the heaven and remote places; and represent things near as afar off, and things afar off as near; making feigned distances. We have also helps for the sight far above spectacles and glasses in use; we have also glasses and means to see small and minute bodies, perfectly and distinctly; as the shapes and colours of small flies and worms, grains, and flaws in gems which cannot otherwise be seen, observations in urine and blood not otherwise to be seen. We make artificial rainbows, halos, and circles about light. We represent also all manner of reflections, refractions, and multiplications of visual beams of objects.

'We have also precious stones, of all kinds, many of them of great beauty and to you unknown; crystals likewise, and glasses of divers kind; and amongst them some of metals vitrificated, and other materials, besides those of which you make glass. Also a number of fossils, and imperfect minerals, which you have not. Likewise load-stones of prodigious virtue: and other rare stones, both natural and artificial.

'We have also sound-houses, where we practice and demonstrate all sounds and their generation. We have harmony which you have not, of quarter-sounds and lesser slides of sounds. Divers instruments of music likewise to you unknown, some sweeter than any you have; with bells and rings that are dainty and sweet. We represent small sounds as great and deep, likewise great sounds, extenuate and sharp; we make divers tremblings and warblings of sounds, which in their original are entire. We represent and imitate all articulate sounds and letters, and the voices and notes of beasts and birds. We have certain helps, which set to the ear do further the hearing greatly; we have also divers strange and artificial echoes, reflecting the voices many times, and as it were tossing it; and some that give back the voice louder than it came, some shriller and some deeper; yea, some rendering the voice, differing in the letters or articulate sound from that they receive. We have all means to convey sounds in trunks and pipes, in strange lines and distances.

'We have also perfume-houses, wherewith we join also practices of taste. We multiply smells which may seem strange: we imitate smells, making all smells to breathe out of other mixtures than those that give them. We make divers imitations of taste likewise, so that they will deceive any man's taste. And in this house we contain also a confiture-house, where we make all sweetmeats, dry and moist, and divers pleasant wines, milks, broths, and salads, far in greater variety than you have.

'We have also engine-houses, where are prepared engines and

instruments for all sorts of motions. There we imitate and practice to make swifter motions than any you have, either out of sour muskets or any engine that you have; and to make them and multiply them more easily and with small force, by wheels and other means, and to make them stronger and more violent than yours are, exceeding your greatest cannons and basilisks. We represent also ordnance and instruments of war and engines of all kinds; and likewise new mixtures and compositions of gunpowder, wild-fires burning in water and unquenchable, also fire-works of all variety, both for pleasure and use. We imitate also flights of birds; we have some degrees of flying in the air. We have ships and boats for going under water and brooking of seas, also swimming-girdles and supporters. We have divers curious clocks and other like motions of return, and some perpetual motions. We imitate also motions of living creatures by images of men, beasts, birds, fishes, and serpents; we have also a great number of other various motions, strange for equality, fineness and subtilty.

'We have also a mathematical-house, where are represented all instruments, as well of geometry as astronomy, exquisitely made.

'We have also houses of deceits of the senses, where we represent all manner of feats of juggling, false apparitions, impostures and illusions, and their fallacies. And surely you will easily believe that we, that have so many things truly natural, which induce admiration, could in a world of particulars deceive the senses if we would disguise those things, and labour to make them more miraculous. But we do hate all impostures and lies, insomuch as we have severely forbidden it to all our fellows, under pain of ignominy and fines, that they do not show any natural work or things adorned or swelling, but only pure as it is, and without all affectation of strangeness.

'These are, my son, the riches of Salomon's House.

'For the several employments and offices of our fellows, we have twelve that sail into foreign countries under the names of other nations (for our own we conceal), who bring us the books and abstracts, and patterns of experiments of all other parts. These we call merchants of light.

'We have three that collect the experiments which are in all books. These we call depredators.

'We have three that collect the experiments of all mechanical arts, and also of liberal sciences, and also of practices which are not brought into arts. These we call mystery-men.

'We have three that try new experiments.

'Such as themselves think good. These we call pioneers or miners.

'We have three that draw the experiments of the former four into titles and tables, to give the better light for the drawing of observations and axioms out of them. These we call compilers. We have three that bend themselves, looking into the experiments of their fellows, and cast about how to draw out of them things of use and practice for man's life and knowledge, as well for works as for plain demonstration of causes, means of natural divinations, and the easy and clear discovery of the virtues and parts of bodies. These we call dowry-men or benefactors.

'Then after divers meetings and consults of our whole number, to consider of the former labours and collections, we have three that take care out of them to direct new experiments, of a higher light, more penetrating into Nature than the former. These we call lamps.

'We have three others that do execute the experiment so directed, and report them. These we call inoculators.

'Lastly, we have three that raise the former discoveries by experiments into greater observations, axioms, and aphorisms. These we call interpreters of Nature.

'We have also, as you must think, novices and apprentices, that the succession of the former employed men do not fail; besides a great number of servants and attendants, men and women. And this we do also: we have consultations, which of the inventions and experiences which we have discovered shall be published, and which not: and take all an oath of secrecy for the concealing of those which we think fit to keep secret: though some of those we do reveal sometime to the state, and some not.

'For our ordinances and rites, we have two very long and fair galleries: in one of these we place patterns and samples of all manner of the more rare and excellent inventions: in the other we place the statues of all principal inventors. There we have the statue of your Columbus, that discovered the West Indies: also the inventor of ships: your Monk that was the inventor of ordnance and of gunpowder: the inventor of music: the inventor of letters: the inventor of printing: the inventor of observations of astronomy: the inventor of works in metal: the inventor of glass: the inventor of silk of the worm: the inventor of wine: the inventor of corn and bread: the inventor of sugars; and all these by more certain tradition than you have. Then we have divers inventors of our own, of excellent works; which since you have not seen, it were too long to make descriptions of them; and besides, in the right understanding of those descriptions you might easily err. For upon every invention of value we erect a statue to the inventor, and give him a liberal and honourable reward. These statues are some of brass, some of marble and touchstone, some of cedar and other special woods gilt and adorned; some of iron, some of silver, some of gold.

'We have certain hymns and services, which we say daily, of laud and thanks to God for His marvellous works. And forms of prayers, imploring His aid and blessing for the illumination of our labours; and turning them into good and holy uses.

'Lastly, we have circuits or visits, of divers principal cities of the kingdom; where as it cometh to pass we do publish such new profitable inventions as we think good. And we do also declare natural divinations of disease, plagues, swarms of hurtful creatures, scarcity, tempest, earthquakes, great inundations, comets, temperature, of the year, and divers other things; and we give counsel thereupon, what the people shall do for the prevention and remedy of them.'

SATIRICAL SCIENCE FICTION

DEAN SWIFT

from *Gulliver's Travels*

From Lucian onwards science fiction has always lent itself to satire, as indeed it still does: a futurist story in a modern US magazine can safely launch a fierce attack, which would hardly be tolerated in any other form, on 'The American way of life'.

Dean Swift (1667–1745) has undergone the same fate as has a modern satirist, George Orwell. 'Like *Animal Farm*, the first two parts of *Gulliver's Travels* (1726), intended as a scathing denunciation of contemporary life, are now delighted in by children, who as much enjoy Swift's giants and pigmies as they do Orwell's enterprising pigs!

Gulliver's third voyage is not so much appreciated by children, nor is it as well known as it deserves among adults. It might almost be regarded as a sardonic repartee to Bacon's *New Atlantis*, for it is a burlesque on the institution which that work helped to create, the Royal Society.

Fantastic as are many of its details, two modern literary critics, Marjorie H. Nicolson and N. B. Mohler,* have shown that almost all of the experiments carried out by the 'protectors' in the Academy of Lagado can be correlated with some of those recorded in the archives of the Royal Society. The panic terror of the Laputan thinkers is similarly based on the apprehensions expressed in Dean Swift's day that the sun might either die out or explode, or that Halley's Comet, whose periodical return had then been recently predicted, might end by colliding with the earth.

(Writing in similar vein, a modern satirist might suggest that we ourselves are obsessed with fears that mankind might be destroyed as the result of a nuclear bombardment in another world war.)

Indeed, some of the entries in the Royal Society's archives,

* The Scientific Background of Swift's Voyage to Laputa and Swift's " Flying Island " in the Voyage to Laputa' (*Annals of Science*).

and of the claims made by its Fellows, seemed to be challenging misunderstanding and satire. When, for example, Robert Hooke declared that thinkers were far too heedless of 'such a trivial thing as a rotten shell', for it could be a far better clue to the earth's history than an ancient coin, it is easy to imagine how the contemporary wits must have sneered! (Though in these days, when such a thing is called a fossil, we feel that the scorn was a little misplaced.)

As for the Flying Island which forms the most interesting feature of the story, this is 'straight' science fiction. As is usual in such work, verisimilitude is given by the 'semi-technical description' which, in the words of Jules Verne's biographer Kenneth Allott, 'comforts and reassures the reader even as he skips the passage'. It is even accompanied by the helpful explicatory diagram also usual in such work – possibly the very first expressly made to illustrate science fiction!

It may be indeed that Swift regarded the mechanism of his Flying Island, even though it was somewhat unlikely, as being quite practicable. Thanks to the researches of William Gilbert, magnetism had aroused deep interest, and the magnets themselves were vaguely credited with far-reaching properties: a gigantic magnet, such as that described by Swift, might be seriously regarded as likely to give even his massive island its ascentional and navigational power.

The whole narrative shows that its author was deeply enough interested in the work of the Royal Society to make an attentive study of its *Proceedings*. It almost suggests the possibility that under happier conditions, instead of burlesquing the Society, Dean Swift might have been one of its Fellows and taken an active part in its work. Then, as he put it, 'being something of a projector himself', he might have devoted his life to applied science or to research. Can it be, indeed, that there is a suggestion of 'sour grapes' in his account of the absent-minded theoreticians of Laputa and the eccentric projects carried out in the Academy of Lagado?

The narrative opens in Dean Swift's usual style as Gulliver explains how he set out on the third of his voyages and how, somewhere east of Japan, he had been captured by pirates and marooned on a desolate island where nothing seemed to await him but death.

I FOUND myself so listless and desponding that I had not the heart to rise, and before I could get spirits enough to creep out of my cave the day was far advanced. I walked a while among the rocks; the sky was perfectly clear, and the sun so hot that I was forced to turn my face from it: when all on a sudden it became obscured, as I thought, in a manner very different from what happens by the interposition of a cloud. I turned back, and perceived a vast opaque body between me and the sun, moving forwards towards the island: it seemed to be about two miles high, and hid the sun six or seven minutes, but I did not observe the air to be much colder, or the sky more darkened, than if I had stood under the shade of a mountain. As it approached nearer over the place where I was, it appeared to be a firm substance, the bottom flat, smooth, and shining very bright from the reflection of the sea below. I stood upon a height about two hundred yards from the shore, and saw this vast body descending almost to a parellel with me, at less than an English mile distance. I took out my pocket-perspective, and could plainly discover numbers of people moving up and down the sides of it, which appeared to be sloping, but what those people were doing, I was not able to distinguish.

The natural love of life gave me some inward motions of joy, and I was ready to entertain a hope that this adventure might some way or other help to deliver me from the desolate place and condition I was in. But at the same time the reader can hardly conceive my astonishment, to behold an island in the air, inhabited by men, who were able (as it should seem) to raise or sink, or put it into a progressive motion, as they pleased. But not being at that time in a disposition to philosophize upon this phenomenon, I rather chose to observe what course the island would take, because it seemed for a while to stand still. Yet soon after it advanced nearer, and I could see the sides of it, encompassed with several gradations of galleries, and stairs at certain intervals, to descend from one to the other. In the lowest gallery I beheld some people fishing with long angling rods, and others looking on. I waved my cap (for my hat was long since worn out) and my handkerchief towards the island; and upon its nearer approach, I called and shouted with the utmost strength of my voice; and then looking circumspectly, I beheld a crowd gather to that side which was most in my view. I found by their pointing towards me and to each other, that they plainly discovered me, although they made no return to my shouting.

But I could see four or five men running in great haste up the stairs to the top of the island, who then disappeared. I happened rightly to conjecture, that these were sent for orders to some person in authority upon this occasion.

The number of people increased, and in less than half an hour the island was moved and raised in such a manner, that the lowest gallery appeared in a parallel of less than a hundred yards distance from the height where I stood. I then put myself into the most supplicating postures, and spoke in the humblest accent, but received no answer. Those who stood nearest over against me seemed to be persons of distinction, as I supposed by their habit. They conferred earnestly with each other, looking often upon me. At length one of them called out in a clear, polite, smooth dialect, not unlike in sound to the Italian; and therefore I returned an answer in that language, hoping at least that the cadence might be more agreeable to his ears. Although neither of us understood the other, yet my meaning was easily known, for the people saw the distress I was in.

They made signs for me to come down from the rock, and go towards the shore, which I accordingly did; and the flying island being raised to a convenient height, the verge directly over me, a chain was let down from the lowest gallery, with a seat fastened to the bottom, to which I fixed myself, and was drawn up by pulleys.

.   .   .   .

At my alighting I was surrounded by a crowd of people, but those who stood nearest seemed to be of better quality. They beheld me with all the marks and circumstances of wonder; neither indeed was I much in their debt, having never till then seen a race of mortals, so singular in their shapes, habits, and countenances. Their heads were all reclined either to the right or the left; one of their eyes turned inward, and the other directly up to the zenith. Their outward garments were adorned with the figures of suns, moons, and stars, interwoven with those of fiddles, flutes, harps, trumpets, guitars, harpsichords, and many other instruments of music, unknown to us in Europe. I observed here and there many in the habit of servants, with a blown bladder fastened like a flail to the end of a short stick which they carried in their hands. In each bladder was a small quantity of dried peas, or little pebbles (as I was afterwards informed). With these bladders they now and then flapped the mouths and ears of those who stood near them, of which practice I could not then conceive the meaning; it seems the minds of these people are so taken up with intense speculation, that they neither can speak, nor attend to the discourses of others, without being roused by some external traction upon the organs of speech and hearing; for which reason those persons who are able to afford it always keep a flapper (the original is *climenole*) in their family, as one of their domestics, nor ever walk abroad or make visits without him. And the business of this officer is, when two or more persons are in company, gently to strike with his bladder the mouth of him who is to speak, and the right ear of him or them to whom the speaker addresseth himself. This flapper is likewise employed diligently to attend his master in his walks, and upon occasion to give him a soft flap on his eyes, because he is always so wrapped up in cogitation, that he is in manifest danger of falling down every precipice, and bouncing his head against every post, and in the streets, of justling others, or being justled himself into the kennel.

It was necessary to give the reader this information, without which he would be at the same loss with me, to understand the proceedings of these people, as they conducted me up the stairs, to the top of the island, and from thence to the royal palace. While we were ascending, they forgot several times what they were about, and left me to myself, till their memories were again roused by their flappers; for they appeared altogether unmoved by the sight of my foreign habit and countenance, and by the shouts of the vulgar, whose thoughts and minds were more disengaged.

At last we entered the palace, and proceeded into the chamber of presence, where I saw the King seated on his throne, attended on each side by persons of prime quality. Before the throne was a large table filled with globes and spheres, and mathematical instruments of all kinds. His Majesty took not the least notice of us, although our entrance was not without sufficient noise, by the concourse of all persons belonging to the court. But he was then deep in a problem, and we attended at least an hour, before he could solve it. There stood by him on each side a young page, with flaps in their hands, and when they saw he was at leisure, one of them gently struck his mouth, and the other his right ear; at which he started like one awaked on the sudden, and looking towards me and the company I was in, recollected the occasion of our coming, whereof he had been informed before. He spoke some words, whereupon immediately a young man with a flap came up to my side, and flapped me gently on the right ear; but I made signs, as well as I could, that I had no occasion for such an instrument; which, as I afterwards found, gave his Majesty and the whole court a very mean opinion of my understanding. The King, as far as I could conjecture, asked me several questions, and I addressed myself to him in all the languages I had. When it was found that I could neither understand nor be understood, I was conducted by the King's order to an apartment in his palace (this prince being distinguished above all his predecessors for his hospitality to strangers), where two servants were appointed to attend me. My dinner was brought, and four persons of quality, whom I remembered to have seen very near the King's person, did me the honour to dine with me. We had two courses of three dishes each. In the first course there was a shoulder of mutton, cut into an equilateral triangle, a piece of beef into a rhomboides, and a pudding into a cycloid. The second course was two ducks, trussed up into the form of fiddles; sausages and puddings resembling flutes and haut-boys, and a breast of veal in the shape of a harp. The servants cut our bread into cones, cylinders, parallelograms, and several other mathematical figures.

While we were at dinner, I made bold to ask the names of several things in their language; and those noble persons, by the assistance of their flappers, delighted to give me answers, hoping to raise my admiration of their great abilities, if I could be brought to converse with them. I was soon able to call for bread and drink, or whatever else I wanted.

After dinner my company withdrew, and a person was sent to teach me the language. He brought with him pen, ink, and paper, and three or four books, giving me to understand by signs, that he was sent to teach me the language. We sat together four hours, in which time I wrote down a great number of words in columns, with the translations over against them. I likewise made a shift to learn several short sentences. For my tutor would order one of my servants to fetch something, to turn about, to make a bow, to sit, or stand, or walk, and the like. Then I took down the sentence in writing. He showed me also in one of his books the figures of the sun, moon, and stars, the zodiac, the tropics, and polar circles, together with the denominations of many figures of planes and solids. He gave me the names and descriptions of all the musical instruments, and the general terms of art in playing on each of them. After he had left me, I placed all my words with their interpretations in alphabetical order. And thus in a few days, by the help of a very faithful memory, I got some insight into their language.

The word, which I interpret the *Flying* or *Floating Island*, is in the original *Laputa*, whereof I could never learn the true etymology. *Lap* in the old obsolete language signifieth *high*, and *untuh*, a *governor*, from which they say by corruption was derived *Laputa*, from *Lapuntuh*. But I do not approve of this derivation, which seems to be a little strained. I ventured to offer to the learned among them a conjecture of my own, that *Laputa* was *quasi lap outed: lap* signifying properly the dancing of the sunbeams in the sea, and *outed*, a wing, which however I shall not obtrude, but submit to the judicious reader.

Those to whom the King had entrusted me, observing how ill I was clad, ordered a tailor to come next morning, and take my measure for a suit of clothes. This operator did his office after a different manner from those of his trade in Europe. He first took my altitude by a quadrant, and then with a rule and compasses described the dimensions and outlines of my whole body, all which he entered upon paper, and in six days brought my clothes very ill made, and quite out of shape, by happening to mistake a figure in the calculation. But my comfort was, that I observed such accidents very frequent, and little regarded.

During my confinement for want of clothes, and by an indisposition that held me some days longer, I much enlarged my dictionary; and when I went next to court, was able to understand many things the King spoke, and to return him some kind of answers. His Majesty had given orders that the island should move north-east and by east, to the vertical point over Lagado, the metropolis of the whole kingdom below upon the firm earth. It was about ninety leagues distant, and our voyage lasted four days and a half. I was not in the least sensible of the progressive motion made in the air by the island. On the second morning about eleven o'clock, the King himself in person, attended by his nobility, courtiers and officers, having prepared all their musical instruments, played on them for three hours without intermission, so that I was quite stunned with the noise; neither could I possibly guess the meaning, till my tutor informed me. He said that the people of the island had their ears adapted to hear the music of the spheres, which always played at certain periods, and the court was now prepared to bear their part in whatever instrument they most excelled.

In our journey towards Lagado, the capital city, his Majesty ordered that the island should stop over certain towns and villages, from whence he might receive the petitions of his subjects. And to this purpose several packthreads were let down with small weights at the bottom. On these packthreads the people strung their petitions, which mounted up directly like the scraps of paper fastened by schoolboys at the end of the string that holds their kite. Sometimes we received wine and victuals from below, which were drawn up by pulleys.

The knowledge I had in mathematics gave me great assistance in acquiring their phraseology, which depended much upon that science and music; and in the latter I was not unskilled. Their ideas are perpetually conversant in lines and figures. If they would, for example, praise the beauty of a woman, or any other animal, they describe it by rhombs, circles, parallelograms, ellipses, and other geometrical terms, or by words of art drawn from music, needless here to repeat. I observed in the King's kitchen all sorts of mathematical and musical instruments, after the figures of which they cut up the joints that were served to his Majesty's table.

Their houses are very ill built, the walls bevil, without one right angle in any apartment, and this defect ariseth from the contempt they bear to practical geometry, which they despise as vulgar and mechanic, those instructions they give being too refined for the intellectuals, of their workmen, which occasions perpetual mistakes. And although they are dexterous enough upon a piece of paper in the management of the rule, the pencil, and the divider, yet in the common actions and behaviour of life, I have not seen a more clumsy, awkward, and unhandy people, nor so slow and perplexed in their conceptions upon all other subjects, except those of mathematics and music. They are very bad reasoners, and vehemently given to opposition, unless when they happen to be of the right opinion, which is seldom their case. Imagination, fancy, and invention, they are wholly strangers to, nor have any words in their language by which those ideas can be expressed; the whole compass of their thoughts and mind being shut up within the two fore-mentioned sciences.

Most of them, and especially those who deal in the astronomical part, have great faith in judicial astrology, although they are ashamed to own it publicly. But what I chiefly admired, and thought altogether unaccountable, was the strong disposition I observed in them towards news and politics, perpetually inquiring into public affairs, giving their judgments in matters of state, and passionately disputing every inch of a party opinion. I have indeed observed the same disposition among most other mathematicians I have known in Europe, although I could never discover the least analogy between the two sciences; unless these people suppose that because the smallest circle hath as many degrees as the largest, therefore the regulation and management of the world requires no more abilities than the handling and turning of a globe. But I rather take this quality to spring from a very common infirmity of human nature, inclining us to be more curious and conceited in matters where we have least concern, and for which we are least adapted either by study of nature.

These people are under continual disquietudes, never enjoying a minute's peace of mind; and their disturbances proceed from causes which very little affect the rest of mortals. Their apprehensions arise from several changes they dread in the celestial bodies. For instance, that the earth, by the continual approaches of the sun towards it, must in course of time be absorbed or swallowed up. That the face of the sun will by degrees be encrusted with its own effluvia, and give no more light to the world. That the earth very narrowly escaped a brush from the tail of the last comet, which would have infallibly reduced it to ashes; and that the next, which they have calculated for one and thirty years hence, will probably destroy us. For if in its perihelion it should approach within a certain degree of the sun (as by their calculations they have reason to dread) it will conceive a degree of heat ten thousand times more intense than that of red-hot glowing iron; and in its absence from the sun, carry a blazing tail ten hundred thousand and fourteen miles long; through which if the earth should pass at the distance of one hundred thousand miles from the nucleus or main body of the comet, it must in its passage be set on fire, and reduced to ashes. That the sun daily spending its rays without any nutriment to supply them, will at last be wholly consumed and annihilated; which must be attended by the destruction of this earth, and of all the planets that receive their light from it.

They are so perpetually alarmed with the apprehensions of these and the like impending dangers, that they can neither sleep quietly in their beds, nor have any relish for the common pleasures or amusements of life. When they meet an acquaintance in the morning, the first question is about the sun's health, how he looked at his setting and rising, and what hopes they have to avoid the stroke of the approaching comet. This conversation they are apt to turn into with the same temper that boys discover, in delighting to hear terrible stories of sprites and hobgoblins, which they greedily listen to, and dare not go to bed for fear.

* * * * * * *

In about a month's time I had made a tolerable proficiency in their language and was able to answer most of the King's questions, when I had the honour to attend him. His Majesty discovered not the least curiosity to inquire into the laws, government, history, religion, or manners of the countries where I had been, but confined his questions to the state of mathematics, and received the account I gave him with great contempt and indifference, though often roused by his flapper on each side.

* * * * * * *

I desired leave of this prince to see the curiosities of the island, which he was graciously pleased to grant, and ordered my tutor to attend me. I chiefly wanted to know to what cause in art or in nature it owed its several motions, whereof I will now give a philosophical account to the reader.

The Flying or Floating Island is exactly circular, its diameter 7838 yards, or about four miles and a half, and consequently contains ten thousand acres. It is three hundred yards thick. The bottom or under surface, which appears to those who view it from below, is one even regular plate of adamant, shooting up to the height of about two hundred yards. Above it lie the several minerals in their usual order, and over all is a coat of rich mould, ten or twelve foot deep. The declivity of the upper surface, from the circumference to the centre, is the natural cause why all the dews and rains which fall upon the island, are conveyed in small rivulets towards the middle, where they are emptied into four large basins, each of about half a mile in circuit, and two hundred yards distant from the centre. From these basins the water is continually exhaled by the sun in the daytime, which effectually prevents their overflowing. Besides, as it is in the power of the monarch to raise the island above the regions of clouds and vapours, he can prevent the falling of dews and rains whenever he pleases. For the highest clouds cannot rise above two miles, as naturalists agree, at least they were never known to do so in that country.

At the centre of the island there is a chasm about fifty yards in diameter, from whence the astronomers descend into a larger dome, which is therefore called *Flandona Gagnole*, or the Astronomer's Cave, situated at the depth of a hundred yards beneath the upper surface of the adamant. In this cave are twenty lamps continually burning, which from the reflection of the adamant cast a strong light into every part. The place is stored with great variety of sextants, quadrants, telescopes, astrolabes, and other astronomical instruments. But the greater curiosity, upon which the fate of the island depends, is a loadstone of a prodigious size, in shape resembling a weaver's shuttle. It is in length six yards, and in the thickest part at least three yards over. This magnet is sustained by a very strong axle of adamant passing through its middle, upon which it plays and is poised so exactly that the weakest hand can turn it. It is hooped round with an hollow cylinder of adamant, four foot deep, as many thick, and twelve yards in diameter, placed horizontally, and supported by eight adamantine feet, each six yards high. In the middle of the concave side there is a groove twelve inches deep, in which the extremities of the axle are lodged, and turned round as there is occasion.

The stone cannot be moved from its place by any force, because the hoop and its feet are one continued piece with that body of adamant which constitutes the bottom of the island.

By means of this loadstone, the island is made to rise and fall, and move from one place to another. For with respect to that part of the earth over which the monarch presides, the stone is endued at one of its sides with an attractive power, and at the other with a repulsive. Upon placing the magnet erect with its attracting end towards the earth, the island descends; but when the repelling extremity points downwards, the island mounts directly upwards. When the position of the stone is oblique, the motion of the island is so too. For in this magnet the forces always act in lines parallel to its direction.

By this oblique motion the island is conveyed to different parts of the monarch's dominions. To explain the manner of its progress, let A B represent a line drawn cross the dominions of Balnibarbi, let the line c d represent the loadstone, of which let d be the repelling end, and c the attracting end, the island being over C: let the stone be placed in the position c d, with its repelling end downwards; then the island will be driven upwards obliquely towards D. When it is arrived at D, let the stone be turned upon its axle, till its attracting end points towards E, and then the island will be carried obliquely toward E: where if the stone be again turned upon its axle it stands in the position E F, with its repelling point downwards, the island will rise obliquely towards F, where by directing the attracting end towards G, the island may be carried to G, and from G to H, by turning the stone, so as to make its repelling extremity point directly downwards. And thus by changing the situation of the stone as often as there is occasion, the island is made to rise and fall by turns in an oblique direction, and by those alternate risings and fallings (the obliquity being not considerable) is conveyed from one part of the dominions to the other.

But it must be observed that this island cannot move beyond the extent of the dominion below, nor can it rise above the height of four miles. For which the astronomers (who have written large systems concerning the stone) assign the following reason: that the magnetic virtue does not extend beyond the distance of four miles, and that the mineral which acts upon the stone in the bowels of the earth, and in the sea about six leagues distance from the shore, is not diffused through the whole globe, but terminated with the limits of the King's dominions; and it was easy from the great advantage of such a superior situation, for a prince to bring under his obedience whatever country lay within the attraction of that magnet.

When the stone is put parallel to the plane of the horizon, the island standeth still; for in that case the extremities of it being at equal distance from the earth, act with equal force, the one in drawing downwards, the other in pushing upwards, and consequently no motion can ensue.

This loadstone is under the care of certain astronomers, who from time to time gave it such positions as the monarch directs. They spend the great part of their lives in observing the celestial bodies, which they do by the assistance of glasses far exceeding ours in goodness. For although they largest telescopes do not exceed three feet, they magnify much more than those of an hundred yards among us, and at the same time show the stars with greater clearness. This advantage hath enabled them to extend their discoveries much farther than our astronomers in Europe; for they have made a catalogue of ten thousand fixed stars, whereas the largest of ours do not contain above one third part of that number. They have likewise discovered two lesser stars, or satellites, which revolve about Mars, whereof the innermost is distant from the centre of the primary planet exactly three of the diameters, and the outermost five; the former revolves in the space of ten hours, and the latter in twenty-one and an half; so that the squares of their periodical times are very near in the same proportion with the cubes of their distance from the centre of Mars, which evidently shows them to be governed by the same law of gravitation, that influences the other heavenly bodies.

They have observed ninety-three different comets, and settled their periods with great exactness. If this be true (and they affiirm it with great confidence), it is much to be wished that their observations were made public, whereby the theory of comets, which at present is very lame and defective, might be brought to the same perfection with other parts of astronomy.

The King would be the most absolute prince in the universe, if he could but prevail on a ministry to join with him; but these having their estates below on the continent, and considering that the office of a favourite hath a very uncertain tenure, would never consent to the enslaving their country.

If any town should engage in rebellion or mutiny, fall into violent factions, or refuse to pay the usual tribute, the King hath two methods of reducing them to obedience. The first and the mildest course is by keeping the island hovering over such a town, and the lands about it, whereby he can deprive them of the benefit of the sun and the rain, and consequently afflict the inhabitants with dearth and diseases. And if the crime deserves it, they are at the same time pelted from above with great stones, against which they have no defence but by creeping into cellars or caves, while the roofs of their houses are beaten to pieces. But if they still continue obstinate, or offer to raise insurrections, he proceeds to the last remedy, by letting the island drop directly upon their heads, which makes a universal destruction both of houses and men. However, this is an extremity to which the prince is seldom driven, neither indeed is he willing to put it in execution, nor dare his ministers advise him to an action, which as it would render them odious to the people, so it would be a great damage to their own estates, which lie all below, for the island is the King's demesne.

But there is still indeed a more weighty reason, why the kings

of this country have been always averse from executing so terrible an action, unless upon the utmost necessity. For if the
town intended to be destroyed should have it in any tall rocks, as
it generally falls out in the larger cities, a situation probably
chosen at first with a view to prevent such a catastrophe; or if
it abound in high spires, or pillars of stone, a sudden fall might
endanger the bottom or under surface of the island, which, although it consists, as I have said, of one entire adamant two
hundred yards thick, might happen to crack by too great a shock,
or burst by approaching too near the fires from the house below, as the backs both of iron and stone will often do in our
chimneys. Of all this the people are well apprised, and understand how far to carry their obstinacy, where their liberty or
property is concerned. And the King, when he is highest pro-
voked, and most determined to press a city to rubbish, orders the
island to descend with great gentleness, out of a pretence of
tenderness to his people, but indeed for fear of breaking the
adamantine bottom; in which case it is the opinion of all their
philosophers that the loadstone could no longer hold it up, and
the whole mass would fall to the ground.

About three years before my arrival among them, while the
King was in his progress over his dominions, there happened
an extraordinary accident which had like to have put a period
to the fate of that monarchy, at least as it is now instituted. Linda-
lino, the second city in the kingdom, was the first his Majesty
visited in his progress. Three days after his departure the inhabitants, who had often complained of great oppressions, shut
the town gates, seized on the governor, and with incredible
speed and labour erected four large towers, one at every corner
of the city (which is an exact square), equal in height to a strong
pointed rock that stands directly in the centre of the city. Upon
the top of each tower, as well as upon the rock, they fixed a
great loadstone, and in case their design should fail, they had
provided a vast quantity of the most combustible fuel, hoping
to burst therewith the adamantine bottom of the island, if the
loadstone project should miscarry.

It was eight months before the King had perfect notice that the
Lindalinians were in rebellion. He then commanded that the
island should be wafted over the city. The people were unani-
mous, and had laid in store of provisions, and a great river runs
through the middle of the town. The King hovered over them
several days to deprive them of the sun and the rain. He ordered

SATIRICAL SCIENCE FICTION 63

many packthreads to be let down, yet not a person offered to send up a petition, but instead thereof very bold demands, the redress of all their grievances, great immunities, the choice of their own governor, and other the like exorbitances. Upon which his Majesty commanded all the inhabitants of the island to cast great stones from the lower gallery into the town; but the citizens had provided against this mischief by conveying their persons and effects into the four towers, and other strong buildings, and vaults underground.

The King being now determined to reduce this proud people, ordered that the island should descend gently within forty yards of the top of the towers and rock. This was accordingly done; but the officers employed in that work found the descent much speedier than usual, and by turning the loadstone could not without great difficulty keep it in a firm position, but found the island inclining to fall. They sent the King immediate intelligence of this astonishing event, and begged his Majesty's permission to raise the island higher; the King consented, a general council was called, and the officers of the loadstone ordered to attend. One of the oldest and expertest among them obtained leave to try an experiment. He took a strong line of an hundred yards, and the island being raised over the town above the attracting power they had felt, he fastened a piece of adamant to the end of his line, which had in it a mixture of iron mineral, of the same nature with that whereof the bottom or lower surface of the island is composed, and from the lower gallery let it down slowly towards the top of the towers. The adamant was not descended four yards, before the officer felt it drawn so strongly downwards that he could hardly pull it back. He then threw down several small pieces of adamant, and observed that they were all violently attracted by the top of the tower. The same experiment was made on the other three towers, and on the rock with the same effect.

This incident broke entirely the King's measures, and (to dwell no longer on other circumstances) he was forced to give the town their own conditions.

I was assured by a great minister that if the island had descended so near the town as not to be able to raise itself, the citizens were determined to fix it for ever, to kill the King and all his servants, and entirely change the government.

. . . .

Although I cannot say that I was ill treated in this island, yet I must confess I thought myself too much neglected, not without some degree of contempt. For neither prince nor people appeared to be curious in any part of knowledge, except mathematics and music, wherein I was far their inferior, and upon that account very little regarded.

On the other side, after having seen all the curiosities of the island, I was very desirous to leave it, being heartily weary of those people. They were indeed excellent in two sciences for which I have great esteem, and wherein I am not unversed; but at the same time so abstracted and involved in speculation, that I never met with such disagreeable companions. I conversed only with women, tradesmen, flappers, and court-pages, during two months of my abode there, by which at last I rendered myself extremely contemptible; yet these were the only people from whom I could ever receive a reasonable answer.

I had obtained by hard study a good degree of knowledge in their language; I was weary of being confined to an island where I received so little countenance, and resolved to leave it with the first opportunity.

. . . .

On the 16th day of February I took leave of his Majesty and the court. The King made me a present to the value of about hundred pounds English, and my protector his kinsman as much more, together with a letter of recommendation to a friend of his in Lagado, the metropolis. The island being then hovering over a mountain about two miles from it, I was let down from the lowest gallery, in the same manner as I had been taken up.

The continent, as far as it is subject to the monarch of the Flying Island, passes under the general name of *Balnibarbi*, and the metropolis, as I said before, is called *Lagado*. I felt some little satisfaction in finding myself on firm ground. I walked to the city without any concern, being clad like one of the natives, and sufficiently instructed to converse with them. I soon found out the person's house to whom I was recommended, presented my letter from his friend the grandee in the island, and was received with much kindness.

. . . .

The sum of his discourse was to this effect. That about forty years ago certain persons went up to Laputa, either upon business or diversion, and after five months' continuance came back with a very little smattering in mathematics, but full of volatile spirits acquired in that airy region. That these persons upon their return began to dislike the management of every thing below, and fell into schemes of putting all arts, sciences, languages, and mechanics upon a new foot. To this end they procured a royal patent for erecting an Academy of Projectors in Lagado; and the humour prevailed so strongly among the people, that there is not a town of any consequence in the kingdom without such an academy. In these colleges the professors contrive new rules and methods of agriculture and building, and new instruments and tools for all trades and manufactures, whereby, as they undertake, one man shall do the work of ten; a palace may be built in a week, of materials so durable as to last for ever without repairing. All the fruits of the earth shall come to maturity at whatever season we think fit to choose, and increase an hundredfold more than they do at present, with innumerable other happy proposals. The only inconvenience is, that none of these projects are yet brought to perfection, and in the mean time, the whole country lies miserably waste, the houses in ruins, and the people without food or clothes. By all which, instead of being discouraged, they are fifty times more violently bent upon prosecuting their schemes, driven equally on by hope and despair; that as for himself, being not of an enterprising spirit, he was content to go on in the old forms, to live in the houses his ancestors had built, and act as they did in every part of life without innovation. That some few other persons of quality and gentry had done the same, but were looked on with an eye of contempt and ill-will, as enemies to art, ignorant, and ill commonwealth's-men, preferring their own ease and sloth before the general improvement of their country.

In a few days we came back to town, and his Excellency, considering the bad character he had in the Academy, would not go with me himself, but recommended me to a friend of his to bear me company thither. My lord was pleased to represent me as a great admirer of projects, and a person of much curiosity and easy belief; which indeed was not without truth, for I had myself been a sort of projector in my younger days.

. . . .

This Academy is not an entire single building, but a continua-
T—C

tion of several houses on both sides of a street, which growing waste was purchased and applied to that use.

I was received very kindly by the Warden, and went for many days to the Academy. Every room hath in it one or more projectors, and I believe I could not be in fewer than five hundred rooms.

The first man I saw was of a meagre aspect, with sooty hands and face, his hair and beard long, ragged and singed in several places. His clothes, shift, and skin were all of the same colour. He had been eight years upon a project for extracting sun-beams out of cucumbers, which were to be put into vials hermetically sealed, and let out to warm the air in raw inclement summer. He told me he did not doubt in eight years more he should be able to supply the Governor's gardens with sunshine at a reasonable rate; but he complained that his stock was low, and entreated me to give him something as an encouragement to ingenuity, especially since this had been a very dear season for cucumbers. I made him a small present, for my lord had furnished me with money on purpose, because he knew their practice of begging from all who go to see them.

I saw another at work to calcine ice into gunpowder, who likewise showed me a treatise he had written concerning the malleability of fire, which he intended to publish.

There was a most ingenious architect who had contrived a new method for building houses, by beginning at the roof, and working downwards to the foundation, which he justified to me by the like practice of those two prudent insects, the bee and the spider.

There was a man born blind, who had several apprentices in his own condition: their employment was to mix colours for painters, which their master taught them to distinguish by feeling and smelling. It was indeed my misfortune to find them at that time not very perfect in their lessons, and the professor himself happened to be generally mistaken: this artist is much encouraged and esteemed by the whole fraternity.

In another apartment I was highly pleased with a projector, who had found a device of ploughing the ground with hogs, to save the charges of ploughs, cattle, and labour. The method is this: in an acre of ground you bury, at six inches distance and eight deep, a quantity of acorns, dates, chestnuts, and other mast or vegetables whereof these animals are fondest; then you drive six hundred or more of them into the field, where in a few days they will root up the whole ground in search of their food, and make it fit for sowing, at the same time manuring it with their dung. It is true, upon experiment they found the charge and trouble very great, and they had little or no crop. However, it is not doubted that this invention may be capable of great improvement.

I went into another room, where the walls and ceiling were all hung round with cobwebs, except a narrow passage for the artist to go in and out. At my entrance he called aloud to me not to disturb his webs. He lamented the fatal mistake the world had been so long in of using silk-worms, while we had such plenty of domestic insects, who infinitely excelled the former, because they understood how to weave as well as spin. And he proposed farther than by employing spiders the charge of dying silks should be wholly saved, whereof I was fully convinced when he showed me a vast number of flies most beautifully coloured, wherewith he fed his spiders, assuring us that the webs would take a tincture from them; and as he had them of all hues, he hoped to fit everybody's fancy, as soon as he could find proper food for the flies, of certain gums, oils, and other glutinous matter to give a strength and consistence to the threads.

There was an astronomer who had undertaken to place a sundial upon the great weathercock on the town-house, by adjusting the annual and diurnal motions of the earth and sun, so as to answer and coincide with all accidental turnings by the wind.

I had hitherto seen only one side of the academy, the other being appropriated to the advancers of speculative learning, of whom I shall say something when I have mentioned one illustrious person more, who is called among them the *universal artist*. He told us he had been thirty years employing his thoughts for the improvement of human life. He had two large rooms full of wonderful curiosities, and fifty men at work. Some were condensing air into a dry tangible substance, by extracting the nitre, and softening marble for pillows and pin-cushions; others, petrifying the hoofs of a living horse to preserve them from foundering. The artist himself was at that time busy upon two great designs; the first, to sow land with chaff, wherein he affirmed the true seminal virtue to be contained, as he demonstrated by several experiments which I was not skilful enough to comprehend. The other was, by a certain composition of gums, minerals, and vegetables outwardly applied, to prevent the growth of wool upon two young lambs; and he hoped in a reasonable time to propagate the breed of naked sheep all over the kingdom.

We crossed a walk to the other part of the Academy, where, as I have already said, the projectors in speculative learning resided.

The first professor I saw was in a very large room, with forty pupils about him. After salutation, observing me to look earnestly upon a frame, which took up the greatest part of both the length and breadth of the room, he said perhaps I might wonder to see him employed in a project for improving speculative knowledge by practical and mechanical operations. But the world would soon be sensible of its usefulness, and he flattered himself that a more noble exalted thought never sprang in any other man's head. Every one knew how laborious the usual method is of attaining to arts and sciences; whereas by his contrivance the most ignorant person at a reasonable charge, and with a little bodily labour, may write books in philosophy, poetry, politics, law, mathematics, and theology, without the least assistance from genius or study. He then led me to the frame, about the sides whereof all his pupils stood in ranks. It was twenty foot square, placed in the middle of the room. The superficies was composed of several bits of wood, about the bigness of a die, but some larger than others. They were all linked together by slender wires. These bits of wood were covered on every square with paper pasted on them, and on these papers were written all the words of their language, in their several moods, tenses, and declensions, but without any order. The professor then desired me to observe, for he was going to set his engine at work. The pupils at his command took each of them hold of an iron handle, whereof there were forty fixed round the edges of the frame, and giving them a sudden turn, the whole disposition of the words was entirely changed. He then commanded six and thirty of the lads to read the several lines softly as they appeared upon the frame; and where they found three or four words together that might make part of a sentence, they dictated to the four remaining boys who were scribes. This work was repeated three or four times, and at every turn the engine was so contrived that the words shifted into new places, as the square bits of wood moved upside down.

Six hours a day the young students were employed in this labour, and the professor showed me several volumes in large folio already collected, of broken sentences, which he intended to piece together, and out of those rich materials to give the world a complete body of all arts and sciences; which, however, might be still improved, and much expedited, if the public would raise a fund for making and employing five hundred such frames in Lagado, and oblige the managers to contribute in common their several collections.

He assured me, that this invention had employed all his thoughts from his youth, that he had emptied the whole vocabulary into his frame, and made the strictest computation of the general proportion there is in books between the numbers of particles, nouns, and verbs, and other parts of speech.

I made my humblest acknowledgement to this illustrious person for his great communicativeness, and promised if ever I had the good fortune to return to my native country, that I would do him justice, as the sole inventor of this wonderful machine; the form and contrivance of which I desired leave to delineate upon paper, as in the figure here annexed. I told him, although it were the custom of our learned in Europe to steal inventions from each other, who had thereby at least this advantage, that it became a controversy which was the right owner, yet I would take such caution, that he should have the honour entire without a rival.

We next went to the school of languages, where three professors sat in consultation upon improving that of their own country.

The first project was to shorten discourse by cutting polysyllables into one, and leaving out verbs and participles, because in reality all things imaginable are but nouns.

The other project was a scheme for entirely abolishing all words whatsoever; and this was urged as a great advantage in point of health as well as brevity. For it is plain that every word we speak is in some degree a diminution of our lungs by corrosion, and consequently contributes to the shortening of our lives. An expedient was therefore offered, that since words are only names for things, it would be more convenient for all men to carry about them such things as were necessary to express the particular business they are to discourse on. And this invention would certainly have taken place, to the great ease as well as health of the subject, if the women, in conjunction with the vulgar and illiterate, had not threatened to raise a rebellion, unless they might be allowed the liberty to speak with their tongues, after the manner of their ancestors; such constant irreconcilable enemies to science are the common people. However, many of the most learned and wise adhere to the new scheme of expressing themselves by things, which hath only this inconvenience attending it, that if a man's business be very great, and of various kinds, he must be obliged in proportion to carry a greater bundle of things upon his back, unless he can afford one or two strong servants to attend him. I have often beheld two of those sages almost sinking under the weight of their packs, like pedlars among us; who, when they met in the streets, would lay down their loads, open their sacks, and hold conversation for an hour together; then put up their implements, help each other to resume their burthens, and take their leave.

But for short conversations a man may carry implements in his pockets and under his arms, enough to supply him, and in his house he cannot be at a loss. Therefore the room where company meet who practice this art, is full of all things ready at hand, requisite to furnish matter for this kind of artificial converse.

Another great advantage proposed by this invention was that it would serve as an universal language to be understood in all civilized nations, whose goods and utensils are generally of the same kind, or nearly resembling, so that their uses might easily be comprehended. And thus ambassadors would be qualified to treat with foreign princes or ministers of state, to whose tongues they were utter strangers.

I was at the mathematical school, where the master taught his pupils after a method scarce imaginable to us in Europe. The proposition and demonstration were fairly written on a thin wafer, with ink composed of a cephalic tincture. This the student was to swallow upon a fasting stomach, and for three days following eat nothing but bread and water. As the water digested, the tincture mounted to his brain, bearing the proposition along with it. But the success hath not hitherto been answerable, partly by some error in the *quantum* or composition, and partly by the perverseness of lads, to whom this bolus is so nauseous, that they generally steal aside, and discharge it upwards before it can operate; neither have they been yet persuaded to use so long an abstinence as the prescription requires.

THE HUMAN MUTANT

ROBERT PALTOCK

from *The Life and Adventures of Peter Wilkins*

Robert Paltock (1697–1767) an attorney of Clement's Inn, is remembered not for his legal work but for his one venture into science fiction. On its appearance in 1751 *Peter Wilkins* gained a very mixed reception: its one reviewer dismissed it as an inferior blend of *Gulliver's Travels* and *Robinson Crusoe*, but it was highly praised by Coleridge, Southey, Charles Lamb, and Leigh Hunt. It has been translated into French and German and formed the basis of a drama and – as one might expect – of several pantomimes.

The story opens in as matter-of-fact a style as *Gulliver* or *Robinson Crusoe*, describing its hero's boyhood and the circumstances in which he left his young wife Patty and went to sea. After being captured by a French privateer he is enslaved by the Portuguese of Angola, but escapes with the aid of a friendly Negro. Having returned to sea he is the only survivor when his vessel is wrecked by collision with some mysterious rock.

Here *Peter Wilkins* ceases to be an exciting adventure story and becomes science fiction. The rock upon which the vessel was wrecked proves to be that traditional peril, a 'magnetic mountain', and on and within the waters round one of its off-shore islands live creatures verging on BEMs. Wilkins has a tussle with an immense eel 'near six feet long and almost as thick as my thigh, whose mouth, throat, and fins, were of a fine scarlet, and the belly was white as snow'; he catches a 'thick fish like a tench but of another colour and much bigger'; and he shoots 'a creature not much unlike our rabbits, but with shorter ears, a longer tail, and hoofed like a kid'.

Having loaded one of the ship's boats with provisions and other stores, he is seeking to return to civilization when he is swept by a current into the immense cavern which traditionally pierces the magnetic mountain. His journey, which takes him about five weeks, ends in an immense lake bordered by a delightful stretch of densely wooded and well-watered country. Here it is the plants that are of unfamiliar type, but some of them, fortunately, are edible.

After the style of Robinson Crusoe, Wilkins takes up residence in a cave, enlarging it by erecting a wooden hut at its entrance. He is perturbed by hearing the sound of mysterious voices, obviously human though he can see nothing to explain them. Then, as is explained in the following extract, he has an encounter first with a remarkable BEM and then with a creature even more remarkable, though BEM is hardly the term one would apply!

A modern writer would probably explain what follows as having been the result of a mutation produced possibly by some experiment into atomic structure or by the explosion of some nuclear weapon. It is unlikely to have occurred to Paltock that any such explanation was either possible or necessary. Few modern authors, however, could have imagined a heroine like the charming Youwarkee, who, as he explains in his dedication, is based in character – though, one presumes, not in physical build – on the Right Honourable Elizabeth, Countess of Northumberland.

THUS finding there were fish to be had, though my present tackle seemed suitable enough to my family, yet could I not rest till I had improved my fishery by enlarging my net; for as it was, even with my late addition, I must either sweep little or no compass of ground, or it would have no bag behind me. Upon this I set to work and shortly doubled the dimensions of it. I had then a mind to try it at the mouth of my rill; so taking it with me the next time I crossed the lake for water, and fastening it to my pole, close by the right side of the rill, I swept a long compass round to the left, and closing the ends, attempted to draw it up in the hollow cut of the rill. But by the time I had gathered up two-thirds of the net, I felt a resistance that quite amazed me. In short, I was not able to stand against the force I felt. Whereupon sitting down in the rill, and clapping my feet to the two sides of it, I exerted all my strength, till finally I became conqueror, and brought up so shocking a monster, that I was just rising to run for my life on the sight of it. But recollecting that the creature was hampered, and could not make so much resistance on the land as in the water, I ventured to drag the net up as far from the rill as my strength and breath would permit me; and then running to the boat for my gun, I returned to the net to examine my prize. Indeed, I had not instantly resolution enough to survey it, and when at length I assumed courage enough to do so, I could not perfectly distinguish the parts, they were so discomposed; but taking hold of one end of the net, I endeavoured to disentangle the thing, and then drawing the net away, a most surprising sight presented itself: the creature reared upright, about three feet high, covered all over with long, black shaggy hair, like a bear, which hung down from his head and neck quite along his back and sides. He had two fins, very broad and large, which, as he stood erect, looked like arms, and these he waved and whirled about with incredible velocity; and though I wondered at first at it, I found afterwards it was the motion of these fins that kept him upright; for I have perceived when they ceased their motion he fell flat on his belly. He had two very large feet, which he stood upon, but could not run, and but barely walk on them, which made me in the less haste to despatch him; and after he had stood upon his feet about four minutes, clapping his fins to his sides, he fell upon his belly.

When I found he could not attack me, I was moving closer to him; but upon sight of my stirring, up he rose again, and whirled his fins about as before so long as he stood. And now I viewed him round, and found he had no tail at all, and that his hinder fins, or feet, very much resembled a large frog's, but were at least ten inches broad, and eighteen long, from heel to toe; and his legs were so short that when he stood upright his breech bore upon the ground. His belly, which he kept towards me, was of an ash-colour, and very broad, as also was his breast. His eyes were small and blue, with a large black sight in the middle, and rather of an oval than round make. He had a long snout like a boar, and vast teeth. Thus having surveyed him near half an hour living, I made him rise up once more and shot him in the breast. He fell, and giving a loud howl, or groan, expired.

I had then time to see what else I had caught; and turning over the net, found a few of the same fish I had taken before, and some others of a flattish make, and one little lump of flesh unformed; which last, by all I could make of it, seemed to be either a spawn or young one of that I had shot.

The great creature was so heavy, I was afraid I must have cut him in pieces to get him to the boat; but with much ado, having stowed the rest, I tumbled him on board. I then filled my watercask and rowed homewards. Being got to land, I was obliged to

bring down my cart, to carry my great beast-fish, as I termed
him, up to the grotto. When I had got him thither, I had a
notion of first tasting, and then, if I liked his flesh, of salting
him down and drying him; so, having flayed him and taken out
the guts and entrails, I boiled a piece of him; but it made such a
blaze that most of the fat ran into the fire, and the flesh proved
so dry and rank that I could no ways endure it.

I then began to be sorry I had taken so much pains for no
profit, and had endangered my net into the bargain (for that
had got a crack or two in the scuffle), and was thinking to throw
away my large but worthless acquisition.

However, as I was now prone to weighing all things, before I
threw it away I resolved to consider a little; whereupon I changed
my mind. Says I, Here is a good warm skin, which, when dry, will
make me a rare cushion. Again, I have for a long while had no
light beside that of the day; but now as this beast's fat makes
such a blaze in the fire, and issues in so great a quantity from
such a small piece as I broiled, why may not I boil a good tallow
or oil out of it? and if I can, I have not made so bad a hand of
my time as I thought for.   In short, I went immediately to work
upon this subject (for I never let a project cool after I had once
started it), and boiled as much of the flesh as the kettle would
hold, and letting it stand to cool, I found it turned out very good
oil for burning; though I confess I thought it would rather have
made tallow. This success quickened my industry; and I repeated the operation till I got about ten quarts of this stuff, which
very well rewarded my labour. After I had extracted as much
oil as I could from the beast-fish, the creature having strongly
impressed my imagination, I conceived a new fancy in relation
to it; and that was, having heard him make a deep, howling
groan at his death, I endeavoured to persuade myself, and at
last verily believed, that the voices I had so often heard in the
dark weather proceeded from numbers of these creatures, divert-
ing themselves in the lake, or sporting together on the shore;
and this thought, in its turn, contributed to ease my apprehensions in that respect.

.   .   .   .

I passed the summer (though I had never yet seen the sun's
body) very much to my satisfaction: partly in the work I have
been describing (for I had taken two more of the beast-fish, and
had a great quantity of oil from them); partly in building me a

himney in my ante-chamber of mud and earth burnt on my
wn hearth into a sort of brick; in making a window at one end
f the abovesaid chamber, to let in what little light would come
hrough the trees when I did not choose to open my door; in
noulding an earthen lamp for my oil; and, finally, in providing
nd laying in stores, fresh and salt (for I had now cured and
ried many more fish), against winter. These, I say, were my
ummer employments at home, intermixed with many agree-
ble excursions. But now the winter coming on, and the days
rowing very short, or indeed there being no day properly speak-
ng, but a kind of twilight, I kept mostly in my habitation,
hough not so much as I had done the winter before, when I had
o light within doors, and slept, or at least lay still, great part of
ny time; for now my lamp was never out. I also turned two of
ny beast-fish skins into a rug to cover my bed, and the third
nto a cushion, which I always sat upon, and a very soft and
varm cushion it made. All this together rendered my life very
asy, yea, even comfortable.

An indifferent person would now be apt to ask, What would
his man desire more than he had? To this I answer, that I was
ontented while my condition was such as I have been describ-
ng; but a little while after the darkness or twilight came on, I frequently heard the voices again; sometimes a few only at a time, as
t seemed, and then again in great numbers. This threw me into
ew fears, and I became as uneasy as ever, even to the degree of
rowing quite melancholy; though, otherwise, I never received
he least injury from anything. I foolishly attempted several
imes, by looking out of my window, to discover what these odd
ounds proceeded from, though I knew it was too dark to see
nything there.

I was now fully convinced, by a more deliberate attention to
hem, that they could not be uttered by the beast-fish, as I had
fore conjectured, but only by beings capable of articulate
peech; but then, what or where they were, it galled me to be
gnorant of.

At length, one night or day, I cannot say which, hearing the
oices very distinctly, and praying very earnestly to be either
elivered from the uncertainty they had put me under, or to have
hem removed from me, I took courage, and arming myself
vith gun, pistols, and cutlass, I went out of my grotto and crept
lown the wood. I then heard them plainer than before, and was
ble to judge from what point of the compass they proceeded.

Hereupon I went forward towards the sound, till I came to the
verge of the wood, where I could see the lake very well by the
dazzle of the water. Thereon, as I thought, I beheld a fleet of
boats, covering a large compass, and not far from the bridge.
was shocked hereat beyond expression. I could not conceive
where they came from, or whither they would go; but supposed
there must be some other passage to the lake than I had found
in my voyage through the cavern, and that for certain they came
that way, and from some place of which as yet I had no manner
of knowledge.

Whilst I was entertaining myself with this speculation, I heard
the people in the boats laughing and talking very merrily, though
I was too distant to distinguish the words. I discerned soon after
all the boats (as I still supposed 'em) draw up, and push for the
bridge; presently after, though I was sure no boat entered the
arch, I saw a multitude of people on the opposite shore all marching towards the bridge; and what was the strangest of all, there
was not the least sign of a boat now left upon the whole lake.
then was in a greater consternation than before; but was still
much more so when I saw the whole posse of people, that as
I have just said were marching towards the bridge, coming over
it to my side of the lake. At this my heart failed, and I was just
going to run to my grotto for shelter; but taking one look more
I plainly discovered that the people, leaping one after another
from the top of the bridge, as if into the water, and then rising
again, flew in a long train over the lake, the lengthways of it
quite out of my sight, laughing, hallooing, and sporting together; so that looking back again to the bridge and on the lake
I could neither see person nor boat, nor anything else, nor hear
the least noise or stir afterwards for that time.

I returned to my grotto brimful of this amazing adventure, be-
moaning my misfortune in being at a place where I was like to
remain ignorant of what was doing about me. For, says I, if
am in a land of spirits, as now I have little room to doubt, there is
no guarding against them. I am never safe, even in my grotto,
for that can be no security against such beings as can sail on
the water in no boats, and fly in the air on no wings, as the case
now appears to me, who can be here and there and wherever they
please. What a miserable state, I say, am I fallen to! I should
have been glad to have had human converse, and to have found
inhabitants in this place; but there being none, as I supposed
hitherto, I contented myself with thinking that I was at least

safe from all those evils mankind in society are obnoxious to. But now, what may be the consequence of the next hour I know not; nay, I am not able to say but whilst I speak, and show my discontent, they may at a distance conceive my thoughts, and be hatching revenge against me for my dislike of them.

The pressure of my spirits inclining me to repose, I laid me down, but could get no rest; nor could all my most serious thoughts, even of the Almighty Providence, give me relief under my present anxiety: and all this was only from my state of uncertainty concerning the reality of what I had heard and seen, and from the earnestness with which I coveted a satisfactory knowledge of those beings who had just taken their flight from me.

I really believe the fiercest wild beast, or the most savage of mankind that had met me, and put me upon my defence, would not have given me half the trouble that then lay upon me; and the more, for that I had no seeming possibility of ever being rid of my apprehensions: so finding, I could not sleep, I got up again; but as I could not fly from myself, all the art I could use with myself was but in vain to obtain me any quiet.

In the height of my distress I had recourse to prayer, with no small benefit; begging that if it pleased not the Almighty Power to remove the object of my fears, at least to resolve my doubts about them, and to render them rather helpful than hurtful to me. I hereupon, as I always did on such occasions, found myself much more placid and easy, and began to hope the best, till I had almost persuaded myself that I was out of danger; and then laying myself down, I rested very sweetly till I was awakened by the impulse of the following dream.

Methought I was in Cornwall, at my wife's aunt's; and inquiring after her and my children, the old gentlewoman informed me, both my wife and children had been dead some time, and that my wife, before her departure, desired her (that is, her aunt) immediately upon my arrival to tell me she was only gone to the lake, where I should be sure to see her, and be happy with her ever after. I then, as I fancied, ran to the lake to find her. In my passage she stopped me, crying, 'Whither so fast, Peter? I am your wife, your Patty.' Methought I did not know her, she was so altered; but observing her voice, and looking more wistfully at her, she appeared to me as the most beautiful creature I ever beheld. I then went to seize her in my arms; but the hurry of my spirits awakened me.

When I got up, I kept at home, not caring even to look out at my door. My dream ran strangely in my head, and I had now nothing but Patty in my mind. 'Oh!' cries I, 'how happy could I be with her, though I had only her in this solitude. Oh! that this was but a reality, and not a dream.' And indeed, though it was but a dream, I could scarce refrain from running to the lake to meet my Patty. But then I checked my folly, and reasoned my-self into some degree of temper again. However, I could not for-bear crying out, 'What, nobody to converse with! Nobody to assist, comfort, or counsel me! This is a melancholy situation indeed.' Thus I ran on lamenting till I was almost weary, when on a sudden I again heard the voices. 'Hark!' says I, 'here they come again. Well, I am now resolved to face them, come life, come death! It is not to be alone I thus dread; but to have com-pany about me, and not know who or what, is death to me worse than I can suffer from them, be they who or what they will.'

During my soliloquy the voices increased, and then by degrees diminished as usual; but I had scarce got my gun in my hand, to pursue my resolution of showing myself to those who uttered them, when I felt such a thump upon the roof of my ante-cham-ber as shook the whole fabric and set me all over into a tremor. I then heard a sort of shriek, and a rustle near the door of my apart-ment; all which together seemed very terrible. But I, having be-fore determined to see what and who it was, resolutely opened my door and leaped out. I saw nobody; all was quite silent, and nothing that I could perceive but my own fears amoving. I went then softly to the corner of the building, and there looking down, by the glimmer of my lamp which stood in the window, I saw something in human shape lying at my feet. I gave the word, 'Who is there?' Still no one answered. My heart was ready to force a way through my side. I was for a while fixed to the earth like a statue. At length, recovering, I stepped in, fetched my lamp, and returning saw the very beautiful face my Patty ap-peared under in my dream; and not considering that it was only a dream, I verily thought I had my Patty before me; but she seemed to be stone dead. Upon viewing her other parts (for I had never yet removed my eyes from her face), I found she had a sort of brown chaplet, like lace, round her head, under and about which her hair was tucked up and twined; and she seemed to me to be clothed in a thin hair-coloured silk garment, which, upon trying to raise her, I found to be quite warm, and therefore hoped there was life in the body it contained. I then took her into my arms, and treading a step backwards with her, I put out my lamp; however, having her in my arms, I conveyed her through the doorway in the dark into my grotto; here I laid her upon my bed, and then ran out for my lamp.

This, thinks I, is an amazing adventure. How could Patty come here, and dressed in silk and whalebone too? Sure that is not the reigning fashion in England now? But my dream said she was dead. Why, truly, says I, so she seems to be. But be it so; she is warm. Whether this is the place for persons to inhabit after death or not, I can't tell (for I see there are people here, though I don't know them); but be it as it will, she feels as flesh and blood; and if I can but bring her to stir and act again as my wife, what matters it to me what she is? It will be a great blessing and comfort to me; for she never would have come to this very spot but for my good.

Top-full of these thoughts, I re-entered my grotto, shut my door and lighted my lamp; when going to my Patty (as I delighted to fancy her), I thought I saw her eyes stir a little. I then set the lamp farther off for fear of offending them if she should look up; and warming the last glass I had reserved of my Madeira, I carried it to her, but she never stirred. I now supposed the fall had absolutely killed her, and was prodigiously grieved; when laying my hand on her breast I perceived the fountain of life had some motion. This gave me infinite pleasure; so, not despairing, I dipped my finger in the wine and moistened her lips with it two or three times, and I imagined they opened a little. Upon this I bethought me, and taking a teaspoon, I gently poured a few drops of the wine by that means into her mouth. Finding she swallowed it, I poured in another spoonful, and another, till I brought her to herself so well as to be able to sit up. All this I did by the glimmering light which the lamp afforded from a distant part of the room, where I had placed it, as I have said, out of her sight.

I then spoke to her, and asked divers questions, as if she had really been Patty and understood me; in return of which she uttered a language I had no idea of, though in the most musical tone, and with the sweetest accent I ever heard. It grieved me I could not understand her. However, thinking she might like to be on her feet, I went to lift her off the bed, when she felt to my touch in the oddest manner imaginable; for while in one respect it was as though she had been cased up in whalebone it was at the same time as soft and warm as if she had been naked.

I then took her in my arms and carried her into my ante-chamber again, where I would fain have entered into conversation, but found she and I could make nothing of it together, unless we could understand one another's speech. It is very strange my dream should have prepossessed me so of Patty, and of the alteration of her countenance, that I could by no means persuade myself the person I had with me was not she; though, upon a deliberate comparison, Patty, as pleasing as she always was to my taste, would no more come up to this fair creature than a coarse ale-wife would to Venus herself.

You may imagine we stared heartily at each other, and I doubted not but she wondered as much as I by what means we came so near each other. I offered her everything in my grotto which I thought might please her; some of which she gratefully received, as appeared by her looks and behaviour. But she avoided my lamp, and always placed her back towards it. I observing that, and ascribing it to her modesty in my company, let her have her will, and took care to set it in such a position myself as seemed agreeable to her, though it deprived me of a prospect I very much admired.

After we had sat a good while, now and then, I may say, chattering to one another, she got up and took a turn or two about the room. When I saw her in that attitude, her grace and motion perfectly charmed me, and her shape was incomparable; but the strangeness of her dress put me to my trumps to conceive either what it was, or how it was put on.

Well, we supped together, and I set the best of everything I had before her, nor could either of us forbear speaking in our own tongue, though we were sensible neither of us understood the other. After supper I gave her some of my cordials, for which she showed great tokens of thankfulness, and often in her way, by signs and gestures, which were very far from being insignificant, expressed her gratitude for my kindness. When supper had been some time over, I showed her my bed and made signs for her to go to it; but she seemed very shy of that, till I showed her where I meant to lie myself, by pointing to myself, then to that, and again pointing to her and to my bed. When at length I had made this matter intelligible to her, she lay down very composedly; and after I had taken care of my fire, and set the things I had been using for supper in their places, I laid myself down too; for I could have no suspicious thoughts or fear of danger from a form so excellent.

I treated her for some time with all the respect imaginable, and never suffered her to do the least part of my work. It was very inconvenient to both of us only to know each other's meaning by signs; but I could not be other wise than pleased to see that she endeavoured all in her power to learn to talk like me. Indeed I was not behindhand with her in that respect, striving all I could to imitate her. What I all the while wondered at was, she never showed the least disquiet at her confinement; for I kept my door shut at first, through fear of losing her, thinking she would have taken an opportunity to run away from me; for little did I then think she could fly.

•   •   •   •   •   •   •

After my new love had been with me a fortnight, finding my water run low, I was greatly troubled at the thought of quitting her any time to go for more; and having hinted it to her, with seeming uneasiness, she could not for a while fathom my meaning; but when she saw me much confused, she came at length, by the many signs I made, to imagine it was my concern for her which made me so; whereupon she expressively enough signified I might be easy, for she did not fear anything happening to her in my absence. On this, as well as I could declare my meaning I entreated her not to go away before my return. As soon as she understood what I signified to her by actions, she sat down, with her arms across, leaning her head against the wall to assure me she would not stir. However, as I had before nailed a cord to the outside of the door, I tied that for caution's sake to the tree, for fear of the worst: but I believe she had not the least design of removing.

I took my boat, net, and water-cask, as usual, desirous of bringing her home a fresh fish dinner, and succeeded so well as to catch enough for several good meals, and to spare. What remained I salted, and found she liked that better than the fresh, after a few days' salting; though she did not so well approve of that I had formerly pickled and dried. As my salt grew very low, though I had been as sparing of it as possible, I now resolved to try making some; and the next summer I effected it.

Thus we spent the remainder of the winter together, till the days began to be light enough for me to walk abroad a little in the middle of them; for I was now under no apprehensions of her leaving me, as she had before this time had so many opportunities of doing so, but never once attempted it.

I must here make one reflection upon our conduct, which you will almost think incredible, viz., that we two, of different sexes, not wanting our peculiar desires, fully inflamed with love to each other, and no outward obstacle to prevent our wishes, should have been together, under the same roof alone for five months, conversing together from morning to night (for by this time she pretty well understood English, and I her language), and yet I should never have clasped her in my arms, or have shown any further amorous desires to her than what the deference I all along paid her could give her room to surmise. Nay, I can affirm that I did not even then know that the covering she wore was not the work of art, but the work of nature, for I really took it for silk; though it must be premised that I had never seen it by any other light than of my lamp. Indeed the modesty of her carriage and sweetness of her behaviour to me had struck into me such a dread of offending her, that though nothing upon earth could be more capable of exciting passion than her charms, I could have died rather than have attempted only to salute her without actual invitation.

When the weather cleared up a little by the lengthening of daylight, I took courage one afternoon to invite her to walk with me to the lake; but she sweetly excused herself from it, whilst there was such a frightful glare of light, as she said; but looking out at the door, told me, if I would not go out of the wood she would accompany me: so we agreed to take a turn only there. I first went myself over the stile of the door, and thinking it rather too high for her, I took her in my arms and lifted her over. But even when I had her in this manner, I knew not what to make of her clothing, it sat so true and close, but seeing by a steadier and truer light in the grove, though a heavy gloomy one, than my lamp had afforded, I begged she would let me know of what silk or other composition her garment was made. She smiled, and asked me if mine was not the same under my jacket. 'No, lady,' says I, 'I have nothing but my skin under my clothes.' – 'Why, what do you mean?' replies she, somewhat tartly; 'but indeed I was afraid that something was the matter by that nasty covering you wear, that you might not be seen. Are you not a glumm?' [a man] – 'Yes,' says I, 'fair creature.' (Here, though you may conceive she spoke part English, part her own tongue, and I the same, as we best understood each other, yet I shall give you our discourse, word for word, in plain English.) 'Then,' says she, 'I am afraid you must have been a very bad man, and have been crashee [slit], which I should be very sorry to hear. I told her I believed we were none of us so good as we might be, but I hoped my faults had not at most exceeded other men's; but I had suffered abundance of hardships in my time; and that at last Providence having settled me in this spot, from whence I had no prospect of ever departing, it was none of the least of its mercies to bring to my knowledge and company the most exquisite piece of all His works, in her, which I should acknowledge as long as I lived. She was surprised at this discourse, and asked me (if I did not mean to impose upon her, and was indeed an ingcrashee [unslit] glumm) why I should tell her I had no prospect of departing hence. 'Have not you,' says she, 'the same prospect that I or any other person has of departing? Sir,' added she, 'you don't do well, and really I fear you are slit, or you would not wear this nasty cumbersome coat (taking hold of my jacket-sleeve), if you were not afraid of showing the signs of a bad life upon your natural clothing.'

I could not for my heart imagine what way there was to get out of my dominions. But certainly, thought I, there must be some way or other, or she would not be so peremptory. And as to my jacket, and showing myself in my natural clothing, I profess she made me blush; and but for shame, I would have stripped to my skin to have satisfied her. 'But, madam,' says I, 'pray pardon me, for you are really mistaken; I have examined every nook and corner of this new world in which we now are, and can find no possible outlet; nay, even by the same way I came in, I am sure it is impossible to get out again.' – 'Why,' says she, 'what outlets have you searched for, or what way can you expect out but the way you came in? And why is that impossible to return by again? If you are not slit, is not the air open to you? Will not the sky admit you to patrole in it, as well as other people? I tell you, sir, I fear you have been slit for your crimes; and though you have been so good to me, that I can't help loving of you heartily for it, yet if I thought you had been slit, I would not, nay, could not, stay a moment longer with you; no, though it should break my heart to leave you.'

I found myself now in a strange quandary, longing to know what she meant by being slit, and had a hundred strange notions in my head whether I was slit or not; for though I knew what the word naturally signified well enough, yet in what manner or by what figure of speech she applied it to me, I had no idea of. But seeing her look a little angrily upon me, 'Pray, madam,' says I, 'don't be offended, if I take the liberty to ask you what you mean by the word crashee [slit] so often repeated by you; for I am an utter stranger to what you mean by it.' – 'Sir,' says she, 'pray answer me first how you came here?' – 'Madam,' replied I, 'will you please to take a walk to the verge of the wood, I will show you the very passage.' – 'Sir,' says she, 'I perfectly know the range of the rocks all round, and by the least description, without going to see them, can tell from which you descended.' – 'In truth,' said I, 'most charming lady, I descended from no rock at all; nor would I for a thousand worlds attempt what could not be accomplished but by my destruction.' – 'Sir,' says she, in some anger, 'it is false, and you impose upon me.' – 'I declare to you,' says I, 'madam, what I tell you is strictly true; I never was near the summit of any of the surrounding rocks, or anything like it; but as you are not far from the verge of the wood, be so good as to step a little farther and I will show you my entrance in hither.' – 'Well,' says she, 'now this odious dazzle of light is lessened, I don't care if I do go with you.'

When we came far enough to see the bridge, 'There, madam,' says I, 'there is my entrance, where the sea pours into this lake from yonder cavern.' – 'It is not possible,' says she; 'this is another untruth; and as I see you would deceive me, and are not to be believed, farewell; I must be gone. But, hold,' says she, 'let me ask you one thing more; that is, by what means did you come through that cavern? You could not have used to have come over the rock?' – 'Bless me, madam!' says I, 'do you think I and my boat could fly? Come over the rock, did you say? No, madam; I sailed from the great sea, the main ocean, in my boat, through that cavern into this very lake here.' – 'What do you mean by your boat?' says she. 'You seem to make two things of your boat you say you sailed with and yourself.' – 'I do so,' replied I; 'for, madam, I take myself to be good flesh and blood, but my boat is made of wood and other materials.' – 'Is it so?' says she. 'And, pray, where is this boat that is made of wood and other materials? – under your jacket?' – 'Lord, madam!' says I, 'you put me in fear that you were angry; but now I hope you only joke with me. What, put a boat under my jacket! No, madam; my boat is in the lake.' – 'What, more untruths?' says she. – 'No, madam,' I replied; 'if you would be satisfied of what I say (every word of which is as true as that my boat now is in the lake), pray walk with me thither and make your own eyes judge what sincerity I speak with.' To this she agreed, it growing dusky; but assured me, if I did not give her good satisfaction, I should see her no more.

We arrived at the lake; and going to my wetdock, 'Now, madam,' says I, 'pray satisfy yourself whether I spake true or no.' She looked at my boat, but could not yet frame a proper notion of it. Says I, 'Madam, in this very boat I sailed from the main ocean through that cavern into this lake; and shall at last think myself the happiest of all men if you continue with me, love me, and credit me; and I promise you I'll never deceive you, but think my life happily spent in your service.' I found she was hardly content yet to believe what I told her of my boat to be true; till I stepped into it, and pushing from the shore, took my oars in my hand, and sailed along the lake by her, as she walked on the shore. At last she seemed so well reconciled to me and my boat, that she desired I would take her in. I immediately did so, and we sailed a good way; and as we returned to my dock I described to her how I procured the water we drank, and brought it to shore in that vessel.

'Well,' says she, 'I have sailed, as you call it, many a mile in my lifetime, but never in such a thing as this. I own it will serve very well where one has a great many things to carry from place to place; but to be labouring thus at an oar when one intends pleasure in sailing, is in my mind a most ridiculous piece of slavery.' – 'Why, pray, madam, how would you have me sail? for getting into the boat only will not carry us this way or that without using some force.' – 'But,' says she, 'pray, where did you get this boat, as you call it?' – 'O madam!' says I, 'that is too long and fatal a story to begin upon now; this boat was made many thousand miles from hence, among a people coal-black, a quite different sort from us; and, when I first had it, I little thought of seeing this country; but I will make a faithful relation of all to you when we come home.' Indeed, I began to wish heartily we were there, for it grew into the night; and having strolled so far without my gun, I was afraid of what I had before seen and heard, and hinted our return; but I found my notion was disagreeable to her, and so I dropped it.

I now perceived and wondered at it, that the later it grew the more agreeable it seemed to her; and as I had now brought her into good-humour again by seeing and sailing in my boat, I was not willing to prevent its increase. I told her, if she pleased, we would land, and when I had docked my boat, I would accompany her where and as long as she liked. As we talked and walked by the lake, she made a little run before me and sprung into it. Perceiving this, I cried out, whereupon she merrily called on me to follow her. The light was then so dim, as prevented my having more than a confused sight of her when she jumped in; and looking earnestly after her, I could discern nothing more than a small boat in the water, which skimmed along at so great a rate that I almost lost sight of it presently; but running along the shore for fear of losing her, I met her gravely walking to meet me, and then had entirely lost sight of the boat upon the lake. 'This,' says she, accosting me with a smile, 'is my way of sailing, which, I perceive, by the fright you were in, you are altogether unacquainted with; and, as you tell me you came from so many thousand miles off, it is possible you may be made differently from me: but, surely we are the part of the creation which has had most care bestowed upon it; and I suspect, from all your discourse, to which I have been very attentive, it is possible you may no more be able to fly than to sail as I do.' – 'No, charming creature,' says I, 'that I cannot, I'll assure you.' She then, stepping to the edge of the lake, for the advantage of a descent before her, sprung up into the air, and away she went farther than my eyes could follow her.

I was quite astonished. 'So,' says I, 'then all is over! all a delusion which I have so long been in! a mere phantom! Better had it been for me never to have seen her, than thus to lose her again! But what could I expect had she stayed? For it is plain she is no human composition. But,' says I, 'she felt like flesh, too, when I lifted her out at the door!' I had but very little time for reflection; for, in about ten minutes after she had left me in this mixture of grief and amazement, she alighted just by me on her feet.

Her return, as she plainly saw, filled me with a transport not to be concealed; and which, as she afterwards told me, was very agreeable to her. Indeed, I was some moment in such an agitation of mind from these unparalleled incidents, that I was like one thunder-struck; but coming presently to myself, and clasping her in my arms with as much love and passion as I was capable of expressing, and for the first time with any desire, – 'Are you returned again, kind angel,' said I, 'to bless a wretch who can only be happy in adoring you? Can it be, that you, who have so many advantages over me, should quit all the pleasures that nature has formed you for, and all your friends and relations, to take an asylum in my arms? But I here make you a tender of all I am able to bestow – my love and constancy.' – 'Come, come,' says she, 'no more raptures; I find you are a wor- thier man than I thought I had reason to take you for, and I beg your pardon for my distrust whilst I was ignorant of your imperfections; but now I verily believe all you have said is true; and I promise you, as you have seemed so much to delight in me, I will never quit you till death, or other as fatal accident shall part us. But we will now, if you choose, go home; for I know you have been some time uneasy in this gloom, though agreeable to me: for, giving my eyes the pleasure of looking eagerly on you, it conceals my blushes from your sight.'

In this manner, exchanging mutual endearments and soft speeches, hand in hand, we arrived at the grotto; where we that night consummated our nuptials, without farther ceremony than mutual solemn engagements to each other; which are, in truth, the essence of marriage, and all that was there and then in our power.

[Not for some years, and till after the birth of several children, was Peter Wilkins able to satisfy a very natural curiosity regard- ing the prowess of his wife Youwarkee.]

I had ever since our marriage been desirous of seeing Youwar- kee fly; but this was the first opportunity I had of it; and indeed the sight was worthy of all the attention I paid it; for I desired her slowly to put herself in proper order for it, that I might make my observation the more accurately; and shall now give you an account of the whole apparatus, though several parts of the description were taken from subsequent views; for it would have been impossible to have made just remarks of everything at that once, especially as I only viewed her back parts then.

I told you before, I had seen her graundee [wings] open, and quite extended as low as her middle; but that being in the grotto by lamplight, I could not take so just a survey as now, when the sort of light we ever had was at the brightest.

She first threw up two long branches or ribs of the whale- bone, as I called it before (and indeed for several of its properties, as toughness, elasticity, and pliableness, nothing I have ever seen can so justly be compared to it), which were joined behind to the upper bone of the spine, and which, when not extended, lie bent over the shoulders on each side of the neck forwards, from whence, by nearer and nearer approaches, they just meet at the lower rim of the belly in a sort of point; but when extended, they stand their whole length above the shoulders, not perpendicularly, but spreading outwards, with a web of the softest and most pliable and springy membrane that can be imagined, in the interstice between them, reaching from their root or joint on the back up above the hinder part of the head, and near half-way their own length; but when closed, the membrane falls down in the middle upon the neck, like a handker-chief. There are also two other ribs rising as it were from the same root, which, when open, run horizontally, but not so long as the others. These are filled up in the interstice between them and the upper ones with the same membrane; and on the lower side of this is also a deep flap of the membrane, so that the arms can be either above or below it in flight, and are always above it when closed. This last rib, when shut, flaps under the upper one, and also falls down with it before to the waist, but is not joined to the ribs below. Along the whole spine-bone runs a strong, flat, broad, grisly cartilage, to which are joined several other of these ribs; all which open horizontally, and are filled in the inter-stices with the above membrane, and are jointed to the ribs of the person just where the plane of the back begins to turn to-wards the breast and belly; and, when shut, wrap the body round to the joints on the contrary side, folding neatly one side over the other. At the lower spine are two more ribs, extended horizontally when open, jointed again to the hips, and long enough to meet the joint on the contrary side cross the belly; and from the hip-joint, which is on the outermost edge of the hip-bone, runs a pliable cartilage quite down the outside of the thigh and leg to the ankle; from which there branch out divers other ribs horizontally also when open, but when closed they encompass the whole thigh and leg, rolling inwards cross the back of the leg and thigh till they reach and just cover the carti-lage. The interstices of these are also filled up with the same membrane. From the two ribs which join to the lower spine-bone, there hangs down a sort of short apron, very full of plaits, from hip-joint to hip-joint, and reaches below the buttocks, half-way or more to the hams. This has also several small limber ribs in it. Just upon the lower spine-joint, and above the apron, as I call it, there are two other long branches, which, when close, extend upon the back from the point they join at below to the shoulders, where each rib has a clasper, which reaching over the shoulders, just under the fold of the uppermost branch or ribs, hold up the two ribs flat to the back like a V, the interstices of which are also filled up with the aforesaid membrane. This last piece, in flight, falls down almost to the ankles, where the two claspers lapping under each leg within-side, hold it very fast; and then also the short apron is drawn up by the strength of the ribs in it, between the thigh forward, and covers the groin as far as the rim of the belly. The whole arms are covered also from the shoulders to the wrist with the same delicate membrane, fastened to ribs of proportionable dimensions, and pointed to a cartilage on the outside in the same manner as on the legs.

It is very surprising to feel the difference of these ribs when open and when closed; for, closed they are as pliable as the finest whalebone, or more so, but when extended, are as strong and stiff as a bone. They are tapering from the roots, and are broader or narrower as best suits the places they occupy, and the stress they are put to, up to their points, which are almost as small as a hair. The membrane between them is the most elastic thing I ever met with, occupying no more space, when the ribs are closed, than just from rib to rib, as flat and smooth as possible; but when extended in some postures, will dilate itself surprisingly.

As soon as my wife had expanded the whole graundee, being upon plain ground, she stooped forward, moving with heavy wriggling motion at first, which put me into some pain for her; but after a few strokes, beginning to rise a little, she cut through the air like lightning, and was soon over the edge of the rock and out of my sight.

It is the most amazing thing in the world to observe the large expansion of this graundee when open; and when closed (as it all is in a moment upon the party's descent) to see it sit so close and compact to the body, as no tailor can come up to it; and then the several ribs lie so justly disposed in the several parts, that instead of being, as one would imagine, a disadvantage to the shape, they make the body and limbs look extremely elegant; and by the different adjustment of their lines on the body and limbs, the whole, to my fancy, somewhat resembles the dress of the old Roman warriors in their buskins; and, to appearance, seems much more noble than any fictitious garb I ever saw, or can frame a notion of to myself.

Though these people, in height, shape, and limb, very much resemble the Europeans, there is yet this difference, that their bodies are rather broader and flatter, and their limbs, though as long and well shaped, are seldom as thick as ours. And this I observed generally in all I saw of them during a long time among them afterwards; but their skin, for beauty and fairness, exceeds ours very much.

VISITORS FROM OUTER SPACE

VOLTAIRE

Micromégas

The progress of astronomy during the seventeenth and eighteenth centuries had suggested the possibility that not merely the moon but the planets and even the fixed stars might be inhabited. This fascinating idea was supported by Bernard le Bovier de Fontenelle (1657–1757) in his *Entretiens sur la Pluralité des Mondes* (1686). This book not only popularized astronomy but actually made it fashionable, introducing it into the *salons* of Paris, where it naturally attracted much attention.

Jean François Arouet de Voltaire (1694–1778) is deservedly famous for his literary and polemical work. Less well known is his very real interest in science, which probably developed during his exile, from 1725 to 1729, in England. Here he met the niece of Sir Isaac Newton, and it was from her that he derived the statement – probably quite well founded – that the theory of gravitation was suggested to Newton from the fall of an apple from a tree.*

Fontenelle's book led Voltaire to speculate ironically: suppose any of the inhabitants of outer space should visit this earth, what would they think of ourselves? Hence his 'philosophical story', *Micromégas* (1752), whose title is derived from the Greek words for 'small' and 'great' and suggests the somewhat ambiguous terms 'a little great man' which he had applied to Fontenelle – who is referred to at the end of the story as the Secretary of the Parisian Academy, and probably as that of the 'Academy of Saturn' mentioned near its beginning.

The expedition described in the story is that led by the French mathematician Pierre Louis Moreau de Maupertuis (1698–1759). In 1736, accompanied by several other savants, he visited

* A cutting from this very tree has, it is claimed, grown into a tree in the grounds of the National Physical Laboratory at Teddington – the only thing in the whole place, it has been said, which the ordinary visitor can understand!

Lapland to measure a degree of the earth's meridian above th
Arctic Circle and to compare it with that obtained in the neigh
bourhood of Paris. His results were published in his work *Sur
Figure de la Terre* (1738); but if his researches were interrupte
in the unceremonious manner narrated by Voltaire he did n
think fit to place this fact on record!

On one of the planets which circle round the star called Siriu
lived an intelligent youth whom I had the honour of meetin
during his last visit to our little ant-heap; he was called Micro
mégas, quite a suitable name for so lofty a person. He was eigl
leagues tall: and by eight leagues I mean twenty-four thousan
geometrical paces each measuring five feet.

Those useful people the algebraists will at once demonstra
that his birthplace must have a circumference twenty-one millic
six hundred thousand times bigger than ours. Our sculptors an
artists will also agree that his waist might have been fifty thou
sand feet round, which seems quite a reasonable proportion.

As for his mind, it was one of the most highly cultivated ther
is; he knew many things and had invented several. He was n
yet two hundred and fifty years old but he had arrived by shee
intelligence at more than fifty of the propositions of Euclid. Bu
he had come into conflict with the authorities; a book he ha
written had been condemned by lawyers who hadn't read i
and he was ordered not to appear at court for another eight hur
dred years.

He was but slightly distressed at being banished from a cou
which was full of nothing but bickering and trivialities. Havin
composed an amusing song against the authorities, who were n
at all put out by it, he began to travel from planet to planet, t
develop his heart and mind, as they say. Those who have travelle
only by post-chaise will doubtless be astonished at the method
of transport they use up there, for we who live on this lump c
mud can never imagine anything we're not familiar with.

Our traveller fully understood the laws of gravitation, and a
the attractive and repulsive forces. He used them so well tha
sometimes by the aid of a ray of sunlight, sometimes by mean
of a comet, he journeyed from world to world, he and his house
hold, like a bird flitting from branch to branch, taking hardl
any time to cross the Milky Way.

In the course of his travels, Micromégas at last reached Saturr

Accustomed as he was to the sight of novelties, when he first realized the small size of this world and its inhabitants he could not keep himself from giving one of those superior smiles which sometimes escape even the wisest. For Saturn is barely nine hundred times bigger than the earth, and its people are nothing but dwarfs, a thousand fathoms tall or thereabouts.

But the Sirian had enough common sense to realize very quickly that to be only six thousand feet tall does not make a thinking being absurd. After the Saturnians had got over their first surprise he very quickly got on good terms with them, and entered into a close friendship with the Secretary of the Academy of Saturn, a singularly intelligent man who had invented nothing but had excellently described other people's inventions very accurately and had also produced some tolerable light verse and heavy calculations.

The two discussed philosophical questions, each lamenting the brevity of life, although that of the Saturnian lasted for seven hundred and fifty thousand of our years and that of the Sirian was seven hundred times as long. This regret, they decided, must be a universal law of nature, for creatures who lived a thousand times longer still murmured against it. 'You can see quite well,' the Saturnian summed it up, 'that we die almost at the moment when we are born, that our existence is a point, our duration an instant, our world an atom. Scarcely has one started to acquire knowledge than death comes before he can use it . . .'

Then they turned to questions of science, and we learn that Sirius is a reddish sun, that its light is made up not of seven primitive colours like ours but of thirty-nine, and that no two suns are alike any more than two human faces are. Having continued their discussion while Saturn circled the sun, they decided to set out together on a philosophical journey.

Our two philosophers were soon ready to soar into the atmosphere of Saturn, with a goodly supply of mathematical instruments. They first landed on its ring, which they found almost flat, as has been inferred by an illustrious inhabitant of our own little world; thence they travelled from moon to moon. Then, as a comet swept past the outermost of these, they jumped on to it with their servants and their instruments. Having made their way among the satellites of Jupiter, they spent a year on the planet itself. There they learned many amazing things, but the records of these have been suppressed by our censors, who think that some of them are going rather too far.

After leaving Jupiter they swept by the planet Mars, which is well known to be five times smaller than the earth, and they saw its two satellites, which have escaped the notice of our astronomers and whose disputed existence is based upon analogy; the philosophers think it would be difficult for Mars, which is so far from the sun, to manage without at least two moons.

Be this as it may, our friends thought the planet so tiny that they feared they wouldn't be able to find anywhere on it to lie down, so they went on their way like two travellers who disdain some wretched village inn to push on to the nearest town. They soon regretted this, however, for they went some distance further without finding anything.

At last they caught sight of a faint gleam: our own earth. Having so recently left Jupiter they thought our planet pitiful, but not wishing to have anything else to regret, they decided to land upon it. They moved along to the tail of their comet; then, finding an aurora borealis all ready, they got into it. Thus they reached earth on the northern shore of the Baltic Sea on the fifth July 1737, new style.

Having rested, they breakfasted off two mountains; then, wanting to reconnoitre the tiny region in which they found themselves, they began exploring it from north to south. The usual Sirian pace being about thirty thousand feet, the Saturnian dwarf had to follow behind panting, taking twelve strides to the other's one, like – if the comparison be allowed – a tiny lap-dog following a captain of the Prussian Royal Guards.

As these foreigners walked rather quickly, they completed their tour of the globe in thirty-six hours; the sun, or rather the earth, does it in a day, but it's easier to turn on one's axis than to walk on one's feet. So there they were back where they had started, after noticing that sea, almost imperceptible to them, which is called the Mediterranean, and that other little pond which, under the name of the Mighty Ocean, surrounds our mole-hill. The dwarf went in it only halfway up his leg, and the other barely moistened the sole of his foot. They did everything they could, as they went hither and thither, to ascertain whether our world were inhabited or not. They stopped, they lay down, they felt everywhere; but their eyes and their hands not being proportionate to the tiny creatures which crawl about here, they did not notice anything, however trivial, to make them suspect that we and our confrères the other inhabitants of this earth have the honour of existing.

The dwarf, who was always a little prone to jump to conclusions, decided at once that there wasn't anybody on the earth. His main reason was that he hadn't seen anybody. Micromégas courteously reminded him that this was an illogical reasoning: 'For,' he said 'your small eyes won't let you see certain stars of the fiftieth magnitude that I can see quite clearly; are you to conclude, therefore, that these stars don't exist?'

'But,' the dwarf protested, 'I've felt carefully.'

'But,' the other reminded him, 'you haven't felt properly.'

'Still,' the dwarf continued, 'this globe is so badly constructed; it's so irregular and its shape looks so absurd! Everything down here seems to be a chaos: look at those tiny rivers, not one of which runs straight, those ponds which are neither round, nor square, nor oval, nor any regular shape; all these tiny pointed grains that this world is bristling with and which keep grazing my feet?' (He meant the mountains.)

'And have you noticed the very shape of this world?' he continued. 'How it's flattened at the poles, how clumsily it circles round the sun, so that its polar regions must be a desert? In fact, what makes me think that there isn't anybody here is that nobody with any sense would care to live here.'

'Well,' conceded Micromégas, 'perhaps they haven't any sense, the people who live here. Still, it doesn't seem as if this world could be made for nothing. It all looks irregular here, you say, because everything's so well laid out in Jupiter and Saturn. Well, perhaps it's for that very reason that things are a little confused here. Haven't I told you that I've always noticed variety wherever I've travelled?'

The Saturnian replied to all these reasons and the argument would never have ended if Micromégas, by some lucky chance, had not broken the thread of his diamond necklace. The diamonds fell to the ground; they were lovely little carats unequal in size, the largest weighing four hundred pounds and the smallest fifty.

The dwarf picked some of them up; and as he raised them to his eyes he noticed that the way in which they were cut had converted them into excellent microscopes. He took one that measured a hundred and sixty feet across and held it in front of one of his pupils, while Micromégas chose another two thousand feet across. They were excellent, but at first they revealed nothing; they had to be adjusted.

At last the visitant from Saturn saw something almost imperceptible moving about under the waters of the Baltic Sea: it was a whale. He hooked it up very skilfully with his little finger; then, placing it on his thumb-nail, he showed it to the Sirian, who for the second time burst into laughter at the minuteness of our earth's inhabitants.

Convinced now that this world is inhabited, the Saturnian at once jumped to the conclusion that it was peopled by whales, and being an excellent logician he now wished to conjecture whence so tiny an atom derived its power of movement and whether it possessed ideas, or any freedom of will. Micromégas was completely at a loss: he scrutinized the animal very patiently, and the result of his investigation was that there was no reason to suppose that it had a soul. The two travellers were thus beginning to think that there existed no intelligence anywhere in our earthy habitation when with the help of the microscope they espied something larger than a whale afloat in the Baltic Sea.

As is well known, there was at that time a covey of philosophers returning from the Arctic Circle, beyond which they had made some hitherto unimagined observations. The papers had reported that their vessel had run aground on the coast of Bothnia, and that they had been saved only with difficulty, but nobody knew the other side of the story. I'm going to explain exactly what happened, without adding anything of my own, which is no small effort for a historian.

Micromégas stretched out his hand very gently to the place where he had noticed the object. Moving two of his fingers backwards and forwards for fear of going wrong, and then opening and closing them, he very cleverly grasped the vessel which was carrying those gentlemen and likewise placed it upon his thumbnail, taking care not to squeeze it hard enough to crush it.

'That's quite a different sort of animal,' commented the dwarf from Saturn, as the Sirian put the supposed animal down in the hollow of his hand.

The ship's crew and the passengers, who fancied that they had been swept along by a storm and were on some sort of rock, at once got busy: the mariners took hold of their casks of wine, threw them on to Micromégas' hand, and jumped after them. The geometers seized their quadrants and their sextants and climbed down on to the Sirian's fingers. The result was that he could feel something moving and tickling his fingers: it was an iron-shod stick that someone had stuck about a foot deep into his index fingers; the prick made him infer that it had emerged from some sort of tiny animal that he'd got hold of. But for the moment he had no suspicion of anything else. The microscope, which was barely powerful enough to enable him to see a whale and a ship, could have no effect with a creature so imperceptible as a man.

What marvellous skill did it not demand from our Sirian philosopher to see the atoms that I've just mentioned! When Leuwenhoek first saw, or thought he could see, the structure of our own bodies, he did not make anything like so amazing a discovery. What a pleasure Micromégas felt in watching the movements of these creatures, in studying their ways, and in following all their proceedings! What exclamations he made! With what delight he thrust one of his microscopes into the hands of his travelling companion!

'I can see them!' they both exclaimed at once. 'Can't you see them carrying those burdens, and stooping down and getting up?' and as they spoke their hands trembled, both with the pleasure of seeing objects so novel and with the fear of losing them.

Micromégas, much more skilful an observer than his dwarf, saw quite clearly that these atoms were talking, and he pointed this out to his companion, who however could not persuade himself that such creatures could exchange ideas. He had the gift of tongues as much as the Sirian; but he couldn't hear those atoms talking, and so he inferred that they couldn't talk.

Anyhow, how could these imperceptible beings have vocal organs, and what could they have to say? In order to talk, one has to think, or something of the sort; but if these creatures thought they would have to have something equivalent to a soul. Well, to attribute the equivalent of a soul to that sort of thing, he thought this absurd.

In reply to the Sirian's arguments, however, he admitted that he no longer dared either believe or deny, he no longer held any opinion at all. 'First we must try to examine these insects,' he added, 'and then we'll theorize about them.'

'That's well spoken,' agreed Micromégas. With a pair of scissors he cut his nails, and with a paring from his thumb-nail he made a sort of vast speaking-trumpet like a great funnel, putting the smaller end to his ear. Its larger end surrounded the ship and its whole crew, and the weakest voice was carried along its circular fibres so that, thanks to his ingenuity, the philosopher from up there could hear quite perfectly the buzzing of our

T—D

insects down here. In quite a short time he was able to distinguish words and even to understand French; so too, though with greater difficulty, could the dwarf.

The travellers' astonishment doubled from instant to instant. They could hear these mites talking quite sensibly and they found this freak of nature quite inexplicable. You may well believe that the Sirian and his dwarf burned with impatience to enter into conversation with these atoms, but they feared that their thunderous voices, and especially that of Micromégas, might deafen them. They would have to reduce its strength, so they thrust into their mouths a sort of small tooth-pick, with the tapering ends just above the vessel.

Then the Sirian took the dwarf on his knee, and the vessel with its crew on one of his nails. He lowered his head and spoke very softly. After taking all these precautions and plenty of others, he began to speak:

'Invisible insects, whom the Creator's hand has pleased to form in the abyss of the infinitely small, I thank Him that He has deigned to disclose to me what seemed to be impenetrable secrets. Perhaps no one else would deign to address you; but I never despise anyone, and I offer you my protection.'

If people have ever been astonished, it was the gentlemen who heard these words. They could not guess who was talking. The ship's chaplain recited an exorcism, the sailors swore, and the philosophers theorized; but in spite of all their efforts they could not imagine whom they had to deal with.

The dwarf from Saturn, who had a softer voice than that of his companion, explained in a few words just whom they had to deal with. He described the journey from Saturn, and introduced them to Monsieur Micromégas. Then, after having condoled with them for being so small, he asked them whether they had always been in this miserable state so little removed from annihilation, what they were doing in a world which seemed to belong to whales, whether they were happy, whether they had offspring, whether they had a soul, and a hundred other questions of the kind.

A logician of the group, bolder than the others and shocked that anyone should doubt whether he had a soul, scrutinized the questioner by levelling the vane on his sextant. He took two observations and then, after taking a third, he replied:

'So you think, Sir, that because you measure a thousand fathoms from your head to your feet you are a . . .'

'A thousand fathoms!' exclaimed the dwarf. 'Merciful heavens! How does he know my height? A thousand fathoms! He isn't an inch out! What, this atom has measured me! He's a geometrician, he knows my height, and I, who can see him only through a microscope, I don't yet know his!'

'Yes, I've measured you,' the doctor assured him, 'and what's more I'll measure your tall companion too.'

The suggestion was accepted. His Excellency stretched himself out at full length, for if he had stood upright his head would have towered above the clouds. Then, by means of a series of triangulations, our philosophers decided that what they could see was certainly a youth a hundred and twenty thousand feet tall.

Then Micromégas said these words: 'I can now see more clearly than ever that one must never judge anything by its apparent size. O God, Thou who has given intelligence to creatures that seem so despicable, the infinitely small costs Thee as little as the infinitely great. So if it is possible that there are creatures even smaller than these, they may none the less have an intelligence greather than that of those magnificent animals which I've seen in the sky, whose foot would alone cover the globe on which I've descended.'

One of the philosophers replied that he might safely believe that there are indeed intelligent beings much smaller than man. He related not all that Virgil has said in his fable about the bees, but what Swammerdam has discovered and Réaumur dissected. He told him too that there are creatures which are to bees what bees are to men, and what the Sirian himself was to those vast animals which he had just described, and what those great animals are to others compared with which they would seem only like atoms.

Gradually the conversation became interesting and Micromégas spoke thus:

'Oh you intelligent atoms, in whom the Eternal Being has been pleased to manifest His power and His skill, no doubt it must be the purest delight that you enjoy on your globe. For as you possess so small a material body that you seem to be nothing but mind, you must spend your lives in loving and thinking, for that is the true life of the mind. Nowhere have I seen true happiness but no doubt it must be here.'

At these words the philosophers shook their heads, and one of them, more frank than the others, replied very solemnly that, except for a few people hardly worth taking into consideration, all the others were an assemblage of fools, villains, and unhappy wretches. 'There's more matter in us than we need,' he explained, 'to do evil, if evil comes from matter, and too much mind, if evil comes from the mind. Realize, for example, that even while I speak there are a hundred thousand fools of our species, covered with hats, who are slaying a hundred thousand others covered with turbans, or who are being slaughtered by them, and that, almost all over the entire earth, things have been so from time immemorial.'

The Sirian trembled, and asked what these horrible quarrels among creatures so despicable could be about.

'What it's about,' the philosopher told him, 'is some lump of mud as big as your heel. It isn't that any one of these men who are going to cut each other's throats cares anything about that lump of mud. It's only to settle whether it is to belong to a certain man who's called *Sultan* or another who's called *Caesar*, I don't know why. Neither the one nor the other has ever seen, or will ever see, that little corner of the earth that all the trouble is about, and hardly one of these animals who are cutting one another's throats has ever seen the animal for whom they're cutting them.'

'Oh, the wretches!' the Sirian exclaimed indignantly. 'Could anyone even imagine so insensate a rage? I've a good mind to take three steps and stamp my foot down three times to crush that whole swarm of preposterous assassins!'

'You can save yourself the trouble,' the other replied. 'They're working quite hard enough for their own destruction. Understand that at the end of ten years hardly the hundredth part of these wretches will be left, that, even if they'd never drawn sword, hunger, weariness or intemperance will sweep them all away.

'Anyhow, they're not the ones who deserve punishment; it's those barbarians behind the scenes, who from the depths of their study, and while they're digesting their meals, order the massacre of a million men and afterwards go and solemnly return thanks for it to God.'

The traveller was touched with pity for the tiny human race, among whom he found such amazing contrasts. 'As you are among the few who are wise,' he told the scientists, 'and as you don't seem to be slaying anybody for money, please tell me what you are busy with.'

'We dissect flies,' the philosopher told him, 'we measure lines, we pile up figures, we agree upon the two or three points we understand, and we argue about the two or three thousand that we don't understand at all.'

It then amused the Sirian and the Saturnian to question these thinking atoms and to find out the points on which they were agreed. 'How far do you make it from the Dog-star to the large star in the Twins?'

'Thirty-two degrees and a half,' they all replied at once.

'How far from here to the moon?'

'Sixty half-diameters of the earth in round numbers.'

'What's the weight of your air?'

This was an attempt to catch them, but they all agreed that the air weighs nine hundred times less than an equal quantity of pure water and nineteen thousand times less than refined gold.

Amazed at these answers, the little dwarf from Saturn was tempted to regard as sorcerers the very people to whom, only a quarter of an hour ago, he had refused a soul.

At last Micromégas addressed them: 'As you know so well what is outside you, no doubt you know even better what is within you. So tell me what your soul is and how you form your ideas.'

As before, the philosophers all spoke at once; but they all held different opinions. The oldest cited Aristotle, the others mentioned such names as Descartes, Leibniz, and Locke. Then an old peripatetic spoke loudly and with an air of confidence: 'The soul is an *entelechy* and it is its own reason for being what it is. That is what Aristotle states expressly . . .'

'I don't understand Greek too well,' put in the giant.

'And neither do I,' admitted the philosophical mite.

'Then why,' the Sirian continued, 'are you citing a certain Aristotle in Greek?'

'Well,' the savant explained, 'it's because one always ought to cite what he doesn't understand at all in a language which he understands even less.'

The follower of Descartes took up the story and said: 'The soul is pure mind, which had received before birth all the metaphysical ideas but which has to go to school after it is born and relearn what it knew so well and what it will never know again.'

'Then it isn't worth while,' commented the animal eight leagues tall, 'for your soul to be so wise before you're born simply to be so ignorant when you've a beard on your chin. But what do you mean by mind?'

'Why ask me that?' demanded the logician, 'I've no idea at all; they say that it isn't matter.'

'But at least you know what matter is?'

'Quite well,' the man replied. 'For example, this stone is grey, it's of such-and-such a shape, it has three dimensions, it's heavy and it's divisible.'

'But,' asked the Sirian, 'this thing which seems to you to be divisible, heavy, and grey, can you tell me just what it is? You can see a few of its attributes, but the depth of the thing, do you know that?'

'No,' admitted the other.

'Then you don't know what matter is.'

Then Monsieur Micromégas, addressing another savant whom he held on his thumb, asked him what his soul was, and what it did.

'Nothing at all,' replied the philosopher, a follower of Malebranche, 'it is God who does everything for me, I do everything in Him, I see everything in Him; it's He who does everything without my having anything to do with it!'

'You might as well not exist,' commented the sage from Sirius. 'And you, my friend,' he asked a follower of Leibnitz who happened to be there, 'What's your soul?'

'It's a needle which shows the hours while my body strikes them; or, perhaps, it's what strikes the hours while my body shows them; or perhaps my soul is the mirror of the universe and body is the mirror's frame; that's quite clear.'

A tiny partisan of Locke was also there, and when at last he was asked: 'I don't know,' he admitted, 'how I think, but I know that I have never thought except by means of my senses. That there may be substances which are both immaterial and intelligent, that's something which I do not doubt; but that it should be impossible for God to endow matter with thought, that's something I doubt very much. I revere the Eternal Power, it is not my place to set bounds to it; I affirm nothing, I content myself with believing that more things are possible than one thinks.'

The animal from Sirius smiled: he did not consider that at all unwise; and the dwarf from Saturn would have kissed the follower of Locke but for the extreme disproportion between them. But unfortunately there happened to be present a tiny animacule in a scholastic cap, who silenced all these philosophic animals by telling them that he had the whole secret, that it was to be found in the *Summa* of Saint Thomas Aquinas.

He looked at the two celestial beings up and down and then informed them that they themselves, their worlds, their suns, their stars, were all made solely for man.

At these words our two travellers let themselves go one after the other in stifling that burst of inextinguishable laughter which, according to Homer characterizes the gods; their shoulders shook, their whole bodies quivered, and in the midst of these convulsions the skin which the Sirian bore on his thumb-nail fell into one of the pockets of the Saturnian's breeches.

The two worthy fellows spent some time in looking for it; at last they found the vessel and readjusted it very carefully.

The Sirian picked up the tiny mites; he spoke to them very kindly, although in the depths of his heart he was somewhat annoyed to see that creatures infinitely small possessed a pride that was almost infinitely great. He promised to compile an admirable philosophical work, written in very small characters, for their use, and added that in that book they would see everything summed up.

And before he left he really did give them that book: it was duly taken to the Academy of Science at Paris.

But when the Secretary opened it he found that all its pages were blank.

'Oh well!' he said, 'I might have known it!'

THE RECALCITRANT ROBOT

MARY SHELLEY

from *Frankenstein*

Hollywood is partly responsible for the mistaken idea that a 'Frankenstein' is some sort of synthetic humanoid monster. Indeed, it may almost come as a shock, in reading the story, to find that the creature which he constructed seems to be nameless, and that Frankenstein is a family name.

Mary Wollstonecraft Shelley (1797–1851), the second wife of the poet Percy Bysshe Shelley, resembled her husband and her own parents in having literary aspirations, her work including a science fiction story whose theme is explained by its title, *The Last Man*.

She owes her fame, however, to her 'horror story', which is also a classic of science fiction, *Frankenstein* (1818). This was written, she explains in a preface, as the result of a discussion between the Shelleys and two literary friends, one of whom was Lord Byron, during which each agreed to write a story of the supernatural. What followed is best explained in her own words.

In the narrative itself an explorer in quest of the North Pole writes a series of interminable letters to his sister, explaining how he had found the hapless Frankenstein among the ice-floes. The two become such good friends that Frankenstein expounds his dread secret, relating how, after prolonged study and deep research into the borderland between alchemy and chemistry he at last acquired the power of bestowing life.

MANY and long were the conversations between Lord Byron and Shelley, to which I was a devout but nearly silent listener. During one of these various philosophical doctrines were discussed, and among others the nature of the principle of life, and whether there was any probability of its ever being discovered and communicated. They talked of the experiments of Dr. Darwin (I speak not of what the Doctor really did, or said that he did, but, as more to my purpose, of what was then spoken of as having been done by him), who preserved a piece of vermicelli in a glass case till by some extraordinary means it began to move with voluntary motion. Not thus, after all, would life be given. Perhaps a corpse would be reanimated; galvanism had given token of such things: perhaps the component parts of a creature might be manufactured, brought together, and endued with vital warmth.

Night waned upon this talk, and even the witching hour had gone by, before we retired to rest. When I placed my head on my pillow I did not sleep, not could I be said to think. My imagination, unbidden, possessed and guided me, gifting the successive images that arose in my mind with a vividness far beyond the usual bounds of reverie. I saw – with shut eyes, but acute mental vision – I saw the pale student of unhallowed arts kneeling beside the thing he had put together. I saw the hideous phantasm of a man stretched out, and then, on the working of some powerful engine, show signs of life, and stir with an uneasy, half vital motion. Frightful must it be; for supremely frightful would be the effect of any human endeavour to mock the stupendous mechanism of the Creator of the world. His success would terrify the artist; he would rush away from his odious handy-work, horror-stricken. He would hope that, left to itself, the slight spark of life which he had communicated would fade; that this thing which had received such imperfect animation, would subside into dead matter; and he might sleep in the belief that the silence of the grave would quench for ever the transient existence of the hideous corpse which he had looked upon as the cradle of life. He sleeps; but he is awakened; he opens his eyes; behold the horrid thing stands at his bedside, opening his curtains, and looking on him with yellow, watery, but speculative eyes.

I opened mine in terror. The idea so possessed my mind that a thrill of fear ran through me, and I wished to exchange the ghastly image of my fancy for the realities around. I see them still; the very room, the dark *parquet*, the closed shutters, with the moonlight struggling through, and the sense I had that the glassy lake and white high Alps were beyond. I could not so easily get rid of my hideous phantom; still it haunted me. I must try to think of something else. I recurred to my ghost story – my tiresome unlucky ghost story! ... On the morrow I announced that I had thought of a story. I began that day with

the words, *It was on a dreary night of November*, making only
a transcript of the grim terrors of my waking dream.

[Frankenstein is in the midst of his confidences to the captain.]

When I found so astonishing a power placed within my hands
I hesitated a long time concerning the manner in which I should
employ it. Although I possessed the capacity of bestowing animation, yet to prepare a frame for the reception of it, with all its
intricacies of fibres, muscles, and veins, still remained a work of
inconceivable difficulty and labour. I doubted at first whether
I should attempt the creation of a being like myself, or one of
simpler organization; but my imagination was too much exalted
by my first success to permit me to doubt of my ability to give
life to an animal as complex and wonderful as man. The materials
at present within my command hardly appeared adequate to so
arduous an undertaking; but I doubted not that I should ulti-
mately succeed. I prepared myself for a multitude of reverses;
my operations might be incessantly baffled, and at last my work
be imperfect: yet, when I considered the improvement which
every day takes place in science and mechanics, I was encouraged
to hope my present attempts would at least lay the foundations
of future success. Nor could I consider the magnitude and com-
plexity of my plan as any argument of its impracticability. It was
with these feelings that I began the creation of a human being.
As the minuteness of the parts formed a great hinderance to my
speed, I resolved, contrary to my first intention, to make the being
of a gigantic stature; that is to say, about eight feet in height,
and proportionably large. After having formed this determina-
tion, and having spent some months in successfully collecting
and arranging my materials, I began.

No one can conceive the variety of feelings which bore me
onwards, like a hurricane, in the first enthusiasm of success.
Life and death appeared to me ideal bounds, which I should first
break through, and pour a torrent of light into our dark world.
A new species would bless me as its creator and source; many
happy and excellent natures would owe their being to me. No
father could claim the gratitude of his child so completely as I
should deserve theirs. Pursuing these reflections, I thought, that
if I could bestow animation upon lifeless matter, I might in
process of time (although I now found it impossible) renew
life where death had apparently devoted the body to corruption.
These thoughts supported my spirits, while I pursued my

undertaking with unremitting ardour. My cheek had grown pale with study, and my person had become emaciated with confinement. Sometimes, on the very brink of certainty, I failed; yet still I clung to the hope which the next day or the next hour might realize. One secret which I alone possessed was the hope to which I had dedicated myself; and the moon gazed on my midnight labours, while, with unrelaxed and breathless eagerness, I pursued nature to her hiding-places. Who shall conceive the horrors of my secret toil, as I dabbled among the unhallowed damps of the grave, or tortured the living animal to animate the lifeless clay? My limbs now tremble and my eyes swim with the remembrance; but then a resistless, and almost frantic, impulse urged me forward; I seemed to have lost all soul or sensation but for this one pursuit. It was indeed but a passing trance that only made me feel with renewed acuteness so soon as, the unnatural stimulus ceasing to operate, I had returned to my old habits. I collected bones from charnel-houses; and disturbed, with profane fingers, the tremendous secrets of the human frame. In a solitary chamber, or rather cell, at the top of the house, and separated from all the other apartments by a gallery and staircase, I kept my workshop of filthy creation: my eye-balls were starting from their sockets in attending to the details of my employment. The dissecting room and the slaughter-house furnished many of my materials; and often did my human nature turn with loathing from my occupation, whilst, still urged on by an eagerness which perpetually increased, I brought my work near to a conclusion.

. . . . . .

It was on a dreary night of November that I beheld the accomplishment of my toils. With an anxiety that almost amounted to agony, I collected the instruments of life around me, that I might infuse a spark of being into the lifeless thing that lay at my feet. It was already one in the morning; the rain pattered dismally against the panes, and my candle was nearly burnt out, when, by the glimmer of the half-extinguished light, I saw the dull yellow eye of the creature open; it breathed hard, and a convulsive motion agitated its limbs.

How can I describe my emotions at this catastrophe, or how delineate the wretch whom with such infinite pains and care I had endeavoured to form? His limbs were in proportion, and I had selected his features as beautiful. Beautiful! – Great God!

His yellow skin scarcely covered the work of muscles and arteries beneath; his hair was of a lustrous black, and flowing; his teeth of a pearly whiteness; but these luxuriances only formed a more horrid contrast with his watery eyes, that seemed almost of the same colour as the dun white sockets in which they were set, his shrivelled complexion and straight black lips.

The different accidents of life are not so changeable as the feelings of human nature. I had worked hard for nearly two years, for the sole purpose of infusing life into an inanimate body. For this I had deprived myself of rest and health. I had desired it with an ardour that far exceeded moderation; but now that I had finished, the beauty of the dream vanished, and breathless horror and disgust filled my heart. Unable to endure the aspect of the being I had created, I rushed out of the room, and continued a long time traversing my bedchamber, unable to compose my mind to sleep. At length lassitude succeeded to the tumult I had before endured; and I threw myself on the bed in my clothes, endeavouring to seek a few moments of forgetfulness. But it was in vain: I slept, indeed, but I was disturbed by the wildest dreams. I thought I saw Elizabeth, in the bloom of health, walking in the streets of Ingolstadt. Delighted and surprised, I embraced her; but as I imprinted the first kiss on her lips, they became livid with the hue of death; her features appeared to change, and I thought that I held the corpse of my dead mother in my arms; a shroud enveloped her form, and I saw the grave-worms crawling in the folds of the flannel. I started from my sleep with horror; a cold dew covered my forehead, my teeth chattered, and every limb became convulsed: when, by the dim and yellow light of the moon, as it forced its way through the window shutters, I beheld the wretch – the miserable monster whom I had created. He held up the curtain of the bed; and his eyes, if eyes they may be called, were fixed on me. His jaws opened, and he muttered some inarticulate sounds, while a grin wrinkled his cheeks. He might have spoken, but I did not hear; one hand was stretched out, seemingly to detain me, but I escaped, and rushed downstairs. I took refuge in the court-yard belonging to the house which I habited; where I remained during the rest of the night, walking up and down in the greatest agitation, listening attentively, catching and fearing each sound as if it were to announce the approach of the demoniacal corpse to which I had so miserably given life.

Oh! no mortal could support the horror of that countenance.

A mummy again endued with animation could not be so hideous as that wretch. I had gazed on him while unfinished; he was ugly then; but when those muscles and joints were rendered capable of motion, it became a thing such as even Dante could not have conceived.

[The monster had in fact come only to express his gratitude; he is for the time being filled with benevolence, and hopes to find human friends. He is so universally regarded with horror, however, that he comes to hate his fabricator and pursues him about Europe like an evil conscience, harassing him and even killing a child, Clerval, whom he (Frankenstein) had loved. Finally he offers – he has mastered human speech – to cease his persecution and to travel to the loneliest parts of earth if only he can be provided with a mate. Frankenstein at last reluctantly agrees and seeks some sequestered place where he can carry out his task.]

Having parted from my friend, I determined to visit some remote spot of Scotland, and finish my work in solitude. I did not doubt but that the monster followed me, and would discover himself to me when I should have finished, that he might receive his companion.

With this resolution I traversed the northern highlands, and fixed on one of the remotest of the Orkneys as the scene of my labours. It was a place fitted for such a work, being hardly more than a rock, whose high sides were continually beaten upon by the waves. The soil was barren, scarcely affording pasture for a few miserable cows, and oatmeal for its inhabitants, which consisted of five persons, whose gaunt and scraggy limbs gave tokens of their miserable fare. Vegetables and bread, when they indulged in such luxuries, and even fresh water, was to be procured from the main land, which was about five miles distant.

On the whole island there were but three miserable huts, and one of these was vacant when I arrived. This I hired. It contained but two rooms, and these exhibited all the squalidness of the most miserable penury. The thatch had fallen in, the walls were unplastered, and the door was off its hinges. I ordered it to be repaired, bought some furniture, and took possession; an incident which would, doubtless, have occasioned some surprise, had not all the senses of the cottagers been benumbed by want and squalid poverty. As it was, I lived ungazed at and unmolested, hardly thanked for the pittance of food and clothes which I gave; so much does suffering blunt even the coarsest sensations of men.

In this retreat I devoted the morning to labour; but in the evening, when the weather permitted, I walked on the stony beach of the sea, to listen to the waves as they roared and dashed at my feet. It was a monotonous yet ever-changing scene. I thought of Switzerland; it was far different from this desolate and appalling landscape. Its hills are covered with vines, and its cottages are scattered thickly in the plains. Its fair lakes reflect a blue and gentle sky; and, when troubled by the winds, their tumult is but as the play of a lively infant, when compared to the roarings of the giant ocean.

In this manner I distributed my occupations when I first arrived; but, as I proceeded in my labour, it became every day more horrible and irksome to me. Sometimes I could not prevail on myself to enter my laboratory for several days; and at other times I toiled day and night in order to complete my work. It was, indeed ,a filthy process in which I was engaged. During my first experiment, a kind of enthusiastic frenzy had blinded me to the horror of my employment; my mind was intently fixed on the consummation of my labour, and my eyes were shut to the horror of my proceedings. But now I went to it in cold blood, and my heart often sickened to the work of my hands.

Thus situated, employed in the most detestable occupation, immersed in a solitude where nothing could for an instant call my attention from the actual scene in which I was engaged, my spirits became unequal; I grew restless and nervous. Every moment I feared to meet my persecutor. Sometimes I sat with my eyes fixed on the ground, fearing to raise them, lest they should encounter the object which I so much dreaded to behold. I feared to wander from the sight of my fellow-creatures, lest when alone he should come to claim his companion.

In the meantime I worked on, and my labour was already considerably advanced. I looked towards its completion with a tremulous and eager hope, which I dared not trust myself to question, but which was intermixed with obscure forebodings of evil, that made my heart sicken in my bosom.

.   .   .   .

I sat one evening in my laboratory; the sun had set, and the moon was just rising from the sea; I had not sufficient light for my employment, and I remained idle, in a pause of consideration of whether I should leave my labour for the night, or hasten its conclusion by an unremitting attention to it. As I sat, a train of reflection occurred to me which led me to consider the effects of what I was now doing. Three years before I was engaged in the same manner, and had created a fiend whose unparalleled barbarity had desolated my heart, and filled it for ever with the bitterest remorse. I was now about to form another being, of whose dispositions I was alike ignorant; she might become ten thousand times more malignant than her mate, and delight, for its own sake, in murder and wretchedness. He had sworn to quit the neighbourhood of man, and hide himself in deserts; but she had not; and she, who in all probability was to become a thinking and reasoning animal, might refuse to comply with a compact made before her creation. They might even hate each other; the creature who already lived loathed his own deformity, and might he not conceive a greater abhorrence for it when it came before his eyes in the female form? She also might turn with disgust from him to the superior beauty of man; she might quit him, and he be again alone, exasperated by the fresh provocation of being deserted by one of his own species.

Even if they were to leave Europe, and inhabit the deserts of the new world, yet one of the first results of those sympathies for which the daemon thirsted would be children, and a race of devils would be propagated upon the earth who might make the very existence of the species of man a condition precarious and full of terror. Had I right, for my own benefit, to inflict this curse upon everlasting generations? I had before been moved by the sophisms of the being I had created; I had been struck senseless by his fiendish threats: but now, for the first time, the wickedness of my promise burst upon me; I shuddered to think that future ages might curse me as their pest, whose selfishness had not hesitated to buy its own peace at the price, perhaps, of the existence of the whole human race.

I trembled, and my heart failed within me; when, on looking up, I saw, by the light of the moon, the daemon at the casement. A ghastly grin wrinkled his lips as he gazed on me, where I sat fulfilling the task which he had allotted to me. Yes, he had followed me in my travels; he had loitered in forests, hid himself in caves, or taken refuge in wide and desert heaths; and he now came to mark my progress, and claim the fulfilment of my promise.

As I looked on him, his countenance expressed the utmost

extent of malice and teachery. I thought with a sensation of madness on my promise of creating another like to him, and trembling with passion, tore to pieces the thing on which I was engaged. The wretch saw me destroy the creature on whose future existence he depended for happiness, and, with a howl of devilish despair and revenge, withdrew.

[Worn out by his privations and distress, Frankenstein passes away, and the captain expresses in his letter home his deep feeling of bereavement. But—]

I am interrrupted. What do these sounds portend? It is midnight; the breeze blows fairly, and the watch on deck scarcely stir. Again; there is a sound of a human voice, but hoarser; it comes from the cabin where the remains of Frankenstein still lies. I must arise and examine. Good night, my sister.

Great God! what a scene has just taken place! I am yet dizzy with the remembrance of it. I hardly know whether I shall have the power to detail it; yet the tale which I have recorded would be incomplete without this final and wonderful catastrophe.

I entered the cabin where lay the remains of my ill-fated and admirable friend. Over him hung a form which I cannot find words to describe; gigantic in stature, yet uncouth and distorted in its proportions. As he hung over the coffin his face was concealed by long locks of ragged hair; but his vast hand was extended, in colour and apparent texture like that of a mummy. When he heard the sound of my approach he ceased to utter exclamations of grief and horror and sprang towards the window. Never did I behold a vision so horrible as his face, of such loathsome and appalling hideousness. I shut my eyes involuntarily and endeavoured to recollect what were my duties with regard to this destroyer. I called on him to stay.

He paused, looking on me with wonder; and, again, turning towards the lifeless form of his creator, he seemed to forget my presence, and every feature and gesture seemed instigated by the wildest rage of some uncontrollable passion.

'That is also my victim!' he exclaimed: 'in his murder my crimes are consummated; the miserable series of my being is wound to its close Oh, Frankenstein! generous and self-devoted being! what does it avail that I now ask thee to pardon me? I, who irretrievably destroyed thee by destroying all thou lovedst. Alas! he is cold, he cannot answer me.'

His voice seemed suffocated; and my first impulse, which

had suggested to me the duty of obeying the dying request of my friend, in destroying his enemy, were now suspended by a mixture of curiosity and compassion. I approached this tremendous being; I dared not again raise my eyes to his face, there was something so scaring and unearthly in his ugliness. I attempted to speak, but the words died away on my lips. The monster continued to utter wild and incoherent self-reproaches. At length I gathered resolution to address him in a pause of the tempest of his passion: 'Your repentance,' I said, 'is now superfluous. If you had listened to the voice of conscience, and heeded the stings of remorse, before you had urged your diabolical vengeance to this extremity, Frankenstein would yet have lived.'

'And do you dream?' said the daemon; 'do you think that I was then dead to agony and remorse? – He,' he continued, pointing to the corpse, 'he suffered not in the consummation of the deed – oh! not the ten-thousandth portion of the anguish that was mine during the lingering detail of its execution. A frightful selfishness hurried me on, while my heart was poisoned with remorse. Think you that the groans of Clerval were music to my ears? My heart was fashioned to be susceptible of love and sympathy; and when wrenched by misery to vice and hatred it did not endure the violence of the change without torture such as you cannot even imagine.

'After the murder of Clerval I returned to Switzerland heart-broken and overcome. I pitied Frankenstein; my pity amounted to horror: I abhorred myself. But when I discovered that he, the author at once of my existence and of its unspeakable torments, dared to hope for happiness; that while he accumulated wretchedness and despair upon me he sought his own enjoyment in feelings and passions from the indulgence of which I was for ever barred, then impotent envy and bitter indignation filled me with an insatiable thirst for vengeance. I recollected my threat and resolved that it should be accomplished. I knew that I was preparing for myself a deadly torture; but I was the slave, not the master, of an impulse which I detested, yet could not disobey. Yet when she died! – nay, then I was not miserable. I had cast off all feeling, subdued all anguish, to riot in the excess of my despair. Evil thenceforth became my good. Urged thus far, I had no choice but to adapt my nature to an element which I had willingly chosen. The completion of my demoniacal design became an insatiable passion. And now it is ended; there is my last victim!'

I was at first touched by the expressions of his misery; yet when I called to mind what Frankenstein had said of his powers of eloquence and persuasion, and when I again cast my eyes on the lifeless form of my friend, indignation was rekindled within me. 'Wretch!' I said, 'it is well that you come here to whine over the desolation that you have made. You throw a torch into a pile of buildings; and when they are consumed you sit among the ruins and lament the fall. Hypocritical fiend! if he whom you mourn still lived, still would he be the object, again would he become the prey, of your accursed vengeance. It is not pity that you feel; you lament only because the victim of your malignity is withdrawn from your power.'

'Oh, it is not thus – not thus,' interrupted the being; 'yet such must be the impression conveyed to you by what appears to be the purport of my actions. Yet I seek not a fellow-feeling in my misery. No sympathy may I ever find. When I first sought it, it was the love of virtue, the feeling of happiness and affection with which my whole being overflowed, that I wished to be participated. But now that virtue has become to me a shadow and that happiness and affection are turned into bitter and loathing despair, in what should I seek for sympathy? I am content to suffer alone while my sufferings shall endure: when I die, I am well satisfied that abhorrence and opprobrium should load my memory. Once my fancy was soothed with dreams of virtue, of fame, and of enjoyment. Once I falsely hoped to meet with beings who, pardoning my outward form, would love me for the excellent qualities which I was capable of unfolding. I was nourished with high thoughts of honour and devotion. But now crime has degraded me beneath the meanest animal. No guilt, no mischief, no malignity, no misery, can be found comparable to mine. When I run over the frightful catalogue of my sins, I cannot believe that I am the same creature whose thoughts were once filled with sublime and transcendent visions of the beauty and the majesty of goodness. But it is even so; the fallen angel becomes a malignant devil. Yet even that enemy of God and man had friends and associates in his desolation; I am alone.

'You, who call Frankenstein your friend, seem to have a knowledge of my crimes and his misfortunes. But in the detail which he gave you of them he could not sum up the hours and months of misery which I endured, wasting in impotent passions. For while I destroyed his hopes, I did not satisfy my own desires. They were for ever ardent and craving; still I desired love and fellowship, and I was still spurned. Was there no injustice in this? Am I to be thought the only criminal when all human kind sinned against me? Why do you not hate Felix who drove his friend from his door with contumely? Why do you not execrate the rustic who sought to destroy the saviour of his child? Nay, these are virtuous and immaculate beings! I, the miserable and the abandoned, am an abortion, to be spurned at, and kicked, and trampled on. Even now my blood boils at the recollection of this injustice.

'But it is true that I am a wretch. I have murdered the lovely and the helpless; I have strangled the innocent as they slept, and grasped to death his throat who never injured me or any other living thing. I have devoted my creator, the select specimen of all that is worthy of love and admiration among men, to misery; I have pursued him even to that irremediable ruin. There he lies, white and cold in death. You hate me; but your abhorrence cannot equal that with which I regard myself. I look on the hands which executed the deed; I think on the heart in which the imagination of it was conceived, and long for the moment when these hands will meet my eyes, when that imagination will haunt my thoughts no more.

'Fear not that I shall be the instrument of future mischief. My work is nearly complete. Neither yours nor any man's death is needed to consummate the series of my being, and accomplish that which must be done; but it requires my own. Do not think that I shall be slow to perform this sacrifice. I shall quit your vessel on the ice-raft which brought me thither, and shall seek the most northern extremity of the globe; I shall collect my funeral pile and consume to ashes this miserable frame, that its remains may afford no light to any curious and unhallowed wretch who would create such another as I have been. I shall die. I shall no longer feel the agonies which now consume me, or be the prey of feelings unsatisfied, yet unquenched. He is dead who called me into being; and when I shall be no more the very remembrance of us both will speedily vanish. I shall no longer see the sun or stars, or feel the winds play on my cheeks. Light, feeling, and sense will pass away; and in this condition must I find my happiness. Some years ago, when the images which this world affords first opened upon me, when I felt the cheering warmth of summer, and heard the rustling of the leaves and the warbling of the birds, and these were all to me, I should have wept to die; now it is my only consolation. Polluted by crimes, and torn by the bitterest remorse, where can I find rest but in death?

'Farewell! I leave you, and in you the last of human kind whom these eyes will ever behold. Farewell, Frankenstein! If thou wert yet alive, and yet cherished a desire of revenge against me it would be better satiated in my life than in my destruction. But it was not so; thou didst seek my extinction that I might not cause greater wretchedness; and if yet, in some mode unknown to me, thou hast not ceased to think and feel, thou wouldst not desire against me a vengeance greater than that which I feel. Blasted as thou wert, my agony was still superior to thine; for the bitter sting of remorse will not cease to rankle in my wounds until death shall close them for ever.

'But soon,' he cried, with sad and solemn enthusiasm, 'I shall die, and what I now feel be no longer felt. Soon these burning miseries will be extinct. I shall ascend my funeral pile triumphantly, and exult in the agony of the torturing flames. The light of that conflagration will fade away; my ashes will be swept into the sea by the winds. My spirit will sleep in peace; or if it thinks, it will not surely think thus. Farewell.'

He sprung from the cabin-window, as he said this, upon the ice-raft which lay close to the vessel. He was soon borne away by the waves and lost in darkness and distance.

THE MENACE OF THE MACHINE

SAMUEL BUTLER

from *Erewhon*

Samuel Butler (1835-1902) held unorthodox views on a variety of subjects, and these led him into violent controversies, the most bitter being with Charles Darwin over the causes of evolution. In 1863 he published an article in a New Zealand paper, and this was largely incorporated into his book *Erewhon: or Over the Range* (1872; the word is pronounced Ĕ:rĕ:whŏn and is of course anagrammatic for 'Nowhere').

In spite of the promise of its opening, the greater part of the book, though it forms an admirable satire on many aspects of contemporary life, can hardly be called science fiction. The sections quoted, however, express a point of view which has not only been developed by many later science fictional writers but, absurd as it seemed a century ago, appears somewhat disquieting today.

The narrator, whose name is given in a later book, *Erewhon Revisited* (1901; it is not science fiction at all), as Higgs, begins by explaining that he was employed on a sheep-station in New Zealand. There he was impressed by the unwillingness of an old native, nicknamed Chowbok, to discuss conditions farther up-country among the hills. Partly by bullying him, partly by bribing him with offers of grog, he at last gets him not indeed to speak but to suggest his meaning, indeed to display it, in a somewhat disquieting manner.

ON a sudden, without a word of warning, he rolled two bales of wool (his strength was very great) into the middle of the floor, and on the top of these he placed another crosswise; he snatched up an empty wool-pack, threw it like a mantle over his shoulders, jumped upon the uppermost bale, and set upon it. In a moment his whole form was changed. His high shoulders dropped; he set his feet close together, heel to heel and toe to

117

toe; he laid his arms and hands close alongside of his body, the palms following his thighs; he held his head high but quite straight, and his eyes stared right in front of him; but he frowned horribly, and assumed an expression of face that was positively fiendish. At the best of times Chowbok was very ugly, but he now exceeded all conceivable limits of the hideous. His mouth extended almost from ear to ear, grinning horribly and showing all his teeth; his eyes glared, though they remained quite fixed, and his forehead was contracted with a most malevolent scowl.

I am afraid my description will have conveyed only the ridiculous side of his appearance; but the ridiculous and the sublime are near, and the grotesque fiendishness of Chowbok's face approached this last, if it did not reach it. I tried to be amused, but I felt a sort of creeping at the roots of my hair and over my whole body, as I looked and wondered what he could possibly be intending to signify. He continued thus for about a minute, sitting bolt upright, as stiff as a stone, and making this fearful face. Then there came from his lips a low moaning like the wind, rising and falling by infinitely small gradations till it became almost a shriek, from which it descended and died away; after that, he jumped down from the bale and held up the extended fingers of both his hands, as one who should say 'Ten', though I did not then understand him.

For myself, I was open-mouthed with astonishment. Chowbok rolled the bales rapidly into their places, and stood before me shuddering as in great fear; horror was written upon his face – this time quite involuntarily – as though the natural panic of one who had committed an awful crime against unknown and superhuman agencies. He nodded his head and gibbered, and pointed repeatedly to the mountains. He would not touch the grog, but after a few seconds he made a run through the wool-shed door into the moonlight; nor did he reappear till next day at dinnertime, when he turned up, looking very sheepish and abject in his civility towards myself.

[Higgs induces Chowbok to lead him up into the hills, but before long the man deserts him. Undeterred, he pushes on alone, and after a hazardous and fatiguing journey he falls asleep beside his camp-fire.]

I dreamed that there was an organ placed in my master's woolshed; the wool-shed faded away, and the organ seemed to grow and grow amid a blaze of brilliant light, till it became like a golden

city upon the side of a mountain, with rows upon rows of pipes
set in cliffs and precipices, one above the other, and in mysterious caverns, like that of Fingal, within whose depths I could see
the burnished pillars gleaming. In the front there was a flight
of lofty terraces, at the top of which I could see a man with his
head buried forward towards a keyboard, and his body swaying
from side to side amid the storm of huge arpeggiod harmonies
that came crashing overhead and round. Then there was one who
touched me on the shoulder, and said, 'Do you not see? it is
Handel'; – but I hardly apprehended, and was trying to scale
the terraces, and get near him, when I awoke, dazzled with the
vividness and distinctness of the dream.

A piece of wood had burned through, and the ends had fallen
into the ashes with a blaze; this, I supposed, had both given me
my dream and robbed me of it. I was bitterly disappointed, and
sitting up on my elbows, came back to reality and my strange
surroundings as best I could.

I was thoroughly aroused – moreover, I felt a foreshadowing
as though my attention were arrested by something more than
the dream, although no sense in particular was as yet appealed
to. I held my breath and waited, and then I heard – was it fancy?
Nay; I listened again and again, and I did hear a faint and
extremely distant sound of music, like that of an Aeolian harp,
borne upon the wind which was blowing fresh and chill from the
opposite mountains.

The roots of my hair thrilled. I listened, but the wind had
died; and, fancying that it must have been the wind itself – no;
on a sudden I remembered the noise which Chowbok had made
in the wool-shed. Yes; it was that.

[After another laborious journey he reaches a glacier which
marks the pass and is shrouded in a cold thin vapour, limiting
visibility to a very few yards.]

I was ... proceeding cautiously through the mist, when I
began to fancy that I saw some objects darker than the cloud
looming in front of me. A few steps brought me nearer, and a
shudder of unutterable horror ran through me when I saw a
circle of gigantic forms, many times higher than myself, up-
standing grim and grey through the veil of cloud before me.

I suppose I must have fainted, for I found myself some time
afterwards sitting upon the ground, sick and deadly cold. There
were the figures, quite still and silent, seen vaguely through the

thick gloom, but in human shape indisputably.

A sudden thought occurred to me, which would have doubtless struck me at once had I not been prepossessed with forebodings at the time that I first saw the figures, and had not the cloud concealed them from me – I mean that they were not living beings, but statues. I determined that I would count fifty slowly, and be sure that the objects were not alive if during that time I could detect no sign of motion.

How thankful was I when I came to the end of my fifty and there had been no movement!

I counted a second time – but again all was still.

I then advanced timidly forward, and in another moment I saw that my surmise was correct. I had come upon a sort of Stonehenge of rude and barbaric figures seated as Chowbok had sat when I questioned him in the wool-shed, and with the same superhumanly malevolent expression upon their faces. They had been all seated, but two had fallen. They were barbarous – neither Egyptian, nor Assyrian, nor Japanese – different from any of these, and yet akin to all. They were six or seven times larger than life, of great antiquity, worn and lichen grown. They were ten in number. There was snow upon their heads and wherever snow could lodge. Each statue had been built of four or five enormous blocks, but how these had been raised and put together is known to those alone who raised them. Each was terrible after a different kind. One was raging furiously, as in pain and great despair; another was lean and cadaverous with famine; another cruel and idiotic, but with the silliest simper that can be conceived – this one had fallen, and looked exquisitely ludicrous in his fall – the mouths of all were more or less open, and as I looked at them from behind, I saw that their heads had been hollowed.

I was sick and shivering with cold. Solitude had unmanned me already, and I was utterly unfit to have come upon such an assembly of fiends in such a dreadful wilderness and without preparation. I would have given everything I had in the world to have been back at my master's station; but that was not to be thought of; my head was failing, and I felt sure that I could never get back alive.

Then came a gust of howling wind, accompanied with a moan from one of the statues above me. I clasped my hands in fear. I felt like a rat caught in a trap, as though I would have turned and bitten at whatever thing was nearest me. The wildness of the wind increased, the moans grew shriller, coming from several statues, and swelling into a chorus. I almost immediately knew what it was, but the sound was so unearthly that this was but little consolation. The inhuman beings into whose hearts the Evil One had put it to conceive these statues, had made their heads into a sort of organ-pipe, so that their mouths should catch the wind and sound with its blowing. It was horrible. However brave a man might be, he could never stand such a concert, from such lips, and in such a place. I heaped every invective upon them that my tongue could utter as I rushed away from them into the mist, and even after I had lost sight of them, and turning my head round could see nothing but the storm-wraiths driving behind me, I heard their ghostly chanting, and felt as though one of them would rush after me and grip me in his hand and throttle me.*

[Beyond the pass Higgs finds a strange civilization; though its people treat him with kindness and consideration they regard him with some suspicion and send him before their magistrates, by whom he is searched.]

But by and by they came to my watch, which I had hidden away in the inmost pocket that I had, and had forgotten when they began their search. They seemed concerned and uneasy as soon as they got hold of it. They then made me open it and show the works; and when I had done so they gave signs of very grave displeasure, which disturbed me all the more because I could not conceive wherein it could have offended them.

I remember that when they first found it I had thought of Paley, and how he tells us that a savage on seeing a watch would at once conclude that it was designed. True, these people were not savages, but I none the less felt sure that this was the conclusion they would arrive at; and I was thinking what a wonderful wise man Archdeacon Paley must have been, when I was aroused by a look of horror and dismay upon the face of the magistrate, a look which conveyed to me the impression that he regarded my watch not as having been designed, but rather as the designer of himself and of the universe; or as at any rate one of the great first causes of all things.

Then it struck me that this view was quite as likely to be

*Higgs adds that after his return to England he was reminded of these statues when he heard one of Handel's compositions for the harpsichord played upon the organ.

taken as the other by a people who had no experience of European civilization, and I was a little piqued with Paley for having led me so much astray; but I soon discovered that I had misinterpreted the expression on the magistrate's face, and that it was one not of fear, but hatred. He spoke to me solemnly and sternly for two or three minutes. Then, reflecting that this was of no use, he caused me to be conducted through several passages into a large room, which I afterwards found was the museum of the town, and wherein I beheld a sight which astonished me more than anything that I had yet seen.

It was filled with cases containing all manner of curiosities – such as skeletons, stuffed birds and animals, carvings in stone (whereof I saw several that were like those on the saddle, only smaller), but the greater part of the room was occupied by broken machinery of all descriptions. The larger specimens had a case to themselves, and tickets with writing on them in a character which I could not understand. There were fragments of steam engines, all broken and rusted; among them I saw a cylinder and piston, a broken fly-wheel, and part of a crank, which was laid on the ground by their side. Again, there was a very old carriage whose wheels, in spite of rust and decay, I could see, had been designed originally for iron rails. Indeed, there were fragments of a great many of our most advanced inventions; but they seemed all to be several hundred years old, and to be placed where they were, not for instruction, but curiosity. As I said before, all were marred and broken.

We passed many cases, and at last came to one in which there were several clocks and two or three old watches. Here the magistrate stopped, and opening the case began comparing my watch with the others. The design was different, but the thing was clearly the same. On this he turned to me and made me a speech in a severe and injured tone of voice, pointing repeatedly to the watches in the case, and to my own; neither did he seem in the least appeased until I made signs to him that he had better take my watch and put it with the others. This had some effect in calming him. I said in English (trusting to tone and manner to convey my meaning) that I was exceedingly sorry if I had been found to have anything contraband in my possession; that I had had no intention of evading the ordinary tolls, and that I would gladly forfeit the watch if my doing so would atone for an unintentional violation of the law. He began presently

to relent, and spoke to me in a kinder manner. I think he saw
that I had offended without knowledge. . . .

[Having been accepted by the Erewhonians and made a number
of friends, Higgs is later introduced to 'a gentleman who had a
great reputation for learning.']

He had heard of my watch and been exceedingly anxious to see
me, for he was accounted the most learned antiquary in Erewhon
on the subject of mechanical lore. We fell to talking upon the
subject, and when I left he gave me a reprinted copy of the work
which brought the revolution about.

It had taken place some five hundred years before my arrival;
people had long become thoroughly used to the change, although
at the time that it was made the country was plunged into the
deepest misery, and a reaction which followed had very nearly
proved successful. Civil war raged for many years, and is said
to have reduced the number of the inhabitants by one half. The
parties were styled the machinists and the anti-machinists, and
in the end, as I have said already, the latter got the victory, treat-
ing their opponents with such unparalleled severity that they
extirpated every trace of opposition.

The wonder was that they allowed any mechanical appliances
to remain in the kingdom, neither do I believe that they would
have done so had not the Professors of Inconsistency and Evasion
made a stand against the carrying of the new principles to their
legitimate conclusions. These Professors, moreover, insisted
that during the struggle the anti-machinists should use every
known improvement in the art of war, and several new weapons,
offensive and defensive, were invented while it was in progress. I
was surprised at there remaining so many mechanical specimens
as are seen in the museums, and at students having rediscovered
their past uses so completely; for at the time of the revolution
the victors wrecked all the more complicated machines, and
burned all treatises on mechanics and all engineers' workshops –
thus, so they thought, cutting the mischief out root and branch,
at an incalculable cost of blood and treasure.

Certainly they had not spared their labour, but work of this
description can never be perfectly achieved; and when, some
two hundred years before my arrival, all passion upon the subject had cooled down, and no one save a lunatic would have
dreamed of reintroducing forbidden inventions, the subject
came to be regarded as a curious antiquarian study, like that of

some long-forgotten religious practices among ourselves. Then came the careful search for whatever fragments could be found, and for any machines that might have been hidden away, and also numberless treatises were written showing what the functions of each rediscovered machine had been; all being done with no idea of using such machinery again, but with the feelings of an English antiquarian concerning Druidical monuments or flint arrowheads.

On my return to the metropolis, during the remaining weeks, or rather days, of my sojourn in Erewhon I made a *résumé* in English of the work which brought about the already mentioned revolution. My ignorance of technical terms has led me doubt-less into many errors, and I have occasionally, where I found translation impossible, substituted purely English names and ideas for the original Erewhonian ones, but the reader may rely on my general accuracy. I have thought it best to insert my trans-lation here.

THE BOOK OF THE MACHINES

[The author begins by discussing the nature of consciousness at some length.]

'Either,' he proceeds, 'a great deal of action that has been called purely mechanical and unconscious must be admitted to contain more elements of consciousness than had been allowed hitherto (and in this case germs of consciousness will be found in many actions of the higher machines) – or (assuming the theory of evolution but at the same time denying the consciousness of vege-table and crystalline action) the race of man has descended from things which had no consciousness at all. In this case there is no *a priori* improbability in the descent of conscious (and more than conscious) machines from those which now exist, except that which is suggested by the apparent absence of anything like a reproductive system in the mechanical king-dom. This absence, however, is only apparent, as I shall presently show.

'Do not let me be misunderstood as living in fear of any actu-ally existing machine; there is probably no known machine which is more than a prototype of future mechanical life. The present machines are to the future as the early Saurians to man. The largest of them will probably greatly diminish in size. Some of the lowest vertebrata attained a much greater bulk than has descended to their more highly organized living representatives, and in like manner a diminution in the size of machines has often attended their development and progress.

'Take the watch, for example; examine its beautiful structure; observe the intelligent play of the minute members which compose it; yet this little creature is but a development of the cumbrous clocks that preceded it; it is no deterioration from them. A day may come when clocks, which certainly at the present time are not diminishing in bulk, will be superseded owing to the universal use of watches, in which case they will become as extinct as ichthyosauri, while the watch, whose tendency has for some years been to decrease in size rather than the contrary, will remain the only existing type of an extinct race.

'But returning to the argument, I would repeat that I fear none of the existing machines; what I fear is the extraordinary rapidity with which they are becoming something very different to what they are at present. No class of beings have in any time past made so rapid a movement forward. Should not that movement be jealously watched, and checked while we can still check it? And is it not necessary for this end to destroy the more advanced of the machines which are in use at present, though it is admitted that they are in themselves harmless?

'As yet the machines receive their impressions through the agency of man's senses; one travelling machine calls to another in a shrill accent of alarm and the other instantly retires; but it is through the ears of the driver that the voice of the one has acted upon the other. Had there been no driver, the callee would have been deaf to the caller. There was a time when it must have seemed highly improbable that machines should learn to make their wants known by sound, even through the ears of man; may we not conceive, then, that a day will come when those ears will be no longer needed, and the hearing will be done by the delicacy of the machine's own construction? – when its language shall have been developed from the cry of animals to a speech as intricate as our own?

'It is possible that by the time children will learn the differential calculus – as they learn now to speak – from their mothers and nurses, or that they may talk in the hypothetical language, and work rule of three sums, as soon as they are born; but this is not probable; we cannot calculate on any corresponding advance in man's intellectual or physical powers which shall be set off against the far greater development which seems in store

for the machines. Some people may say that man's moral influence will suffice to rule them; but I cannot think it will ever
be safe to repose much trust in the moral sense of any machine.'

[The writer becomes so obscure that Higgs has to miss several
pages but then resumes his argument.]

'It can be answered that even though machines should hear
never so well and speak never so wisely, they will still always do
the one or the other for our advantage, not their own; that man
will be the ruling spirit and the machine the servant; that as
soon as a machine fails to discharge the service which man expects from it, it is doomed to extinction; that the machines
stand to man simply in the relation of lower animals, the vapour-
engine itself being only a more economical kind of horse; so that
instead of being likely to be developed into a higher kind of life
than man's, they owe their very existence and progress to their
power of ministering to human wants, and must therefore both
now and ever be man's inferiors.

'This is all very well. But the servant glides by imperceptible
approaches into the master; and we have come to such a pass
that, even now, man must suffer terribly on ceasing to benefit
the machines. If all machines were to be annihilated at one
moment, so that not a knife nor lever nor rag of clothing nor
anything whatsoever were left to man but his bare body alone
that he was born with, and if all knowledge of mechanical laws
were taken from him so that he could make no more machines,
and all machine-made food destroyed so that the race of man
should be left as it were naked upon the desert island, we should
become extinct in six weeks. A few miserable individuals might
linger, but even these in a year or two would become worse than
monkeys. Man's very soul is due to the machines; it is a machine-
made thing; he thinks as he thinks, and feels as he feels, through
the work that machines have wrought upon him, and their existence is quite as much a *sine quâ non* for his, as his for theirs. This
fact precludes us from proposing the complete annihilation of
machinery, but surely it indicates that we should destroy as
many of them as we can possibly dispense with, lest they should
tyrannize over us even more completely.

'True, from a low materialistic point of view, it would seem
that those thrive best who use machinery wherever its use is
possible with profit; but this is the art of the machines – they
serve that they may rule. They bear no malice towards man for

destroying a whole race of them provided he creates a better instead; on the contrary, they reward him liberally for having hastened their development. It is for neglecting them that he incurs their wrath, or for using inferior machines, or for not making sufficient exertions to invent new ones, or for destroying them without replacing them; yet these are the very things we ought to do, and do quickly; for though our rebellion against their infant power will cause infinite suffering, what will not things come to, if that rebellion is delayed?

'They have preyed upon man's grovelling preference for his material over his spiritual interests, and have betrayed him into supplying that element of struggle and warfare without which no race can advance. The lower animals progress because they struggle with one another; the weaker die, the stronger breed and transmit their strength. The machines being of themselves unable to struggle, have got man to do their struggling for them; as long as he fulfils this function duly, all goes well with him – at least he thinks so; but the moment he fails to do his best for the advancement of machinery by encouraging the good and destroying the bad, he is left behind in the race of competition; and this means that he will be made uncomfortable in a variety of ways, and perhaps die.

'So that even now the machines will only serve on condition of being served, and that too upon their own terms; the moment their terms are not complied with, they jib, and either smash both themselves and all whom they can reach, or turn churlish and refuse to work at all. How many men at this hour are living in a state of bondage to the machines? How many spend their whole lives, from the cradle to the grave, in tending them by night and day? Is it not plain that the machines are gaining ground upon us, when we reflect on the increasing number of those who are bound down to them as slaves, and of those who devote their whole souls to the advancement of the mechanical kingdom?

'The vapour-engine must be fed with food and consume it by fire even as man consumes it; it supports its combustion by air as man supports it; it has a pulse and circulation as man has. It may be granted that man's body is as yet the more versatile of the two, but then man's body is an older thing; give the vapour-engine but half the time that man has had, give it also a continuance of our present infatuation, and what may it not ere long attain to?

'There are certain functions indeed of the vapour-engine which will probably remain unchanged for myriads of years – which in fact will perhaps survive when the use of vapour has been superseded; the piston and cylinder, the beam, the fly-wheel, and other parts of the machine will probably be permanent, just as we see that man and many of the lower animals share like modes of eating, drinking, and sleeping; thus they have hearts which beat as ours, veins and arteries, eyes, ears, and noses; they sigh even in their sleep, and weep and yawn; they are affected by their children; they feel pleasure and pain, hope, fear, anger, shame; they have memory and prescience; they know that if certain things happen to them they will die, and they fear death as much as we do; they communicate their thoughts to one another, and some of them deliberately act in concert. The comparison of similarities is endless; I only make it because some may say that since the vapour-engine is not likely to be improved in the main particulars, it is unlikely to be henceforward extensively modified at all. This is too good to be true; it will be modified and suited for an infinite variety of purposes, as much as man has been modified so as to exceed the brutes in skill.

'In the meantime the stoker is almost as much a cook for his engine as our own cooks for ourselves. Consider also the colliers and pitmen and coal merchants and coal trains, and the men who drive them, and the ships that carry coals – what an army of servants do the machines thus employ! Are there not probably more men engaged in tending machinery than in tending men? Do not machines eat as it were by mannery? Are we not ourselves creating our successors in the supremacy of the earth? daily adding to the beauty and delicacy of their organization, daily giving them greater skill and supplying more and more of that self-regulating, self-acting power which will be better than any intellect?

'What a new thing it is for a machine to feed at all! The plough, the spade, and the cart must eat through man's stomach; the fuel that sets them going must burn in the furnace of a man or of horses. Man must consume bread and meat or he cannot dig; the bread and meat are the fuel which drive the spade. If a plough be drawn by horses, the power is supplied by grass or beans or oats, which being burnt in the belly of the cattle give the power of working; without this fuel the work would cease, as an engine would stop if its furnaces were to go out.

'A man of science has demonstrated "that no animal has the power of originating mechanical energy, but that all the work done in its life by any animal, and all the heat that has been emitted from it, and the heat which would be obtained by burning the combustible matter which had been lost from its body during life, and by burning its body after death, make up altogether an exact equivalent to the heat which would be obtained by burning as much food as it has used during its life, and an amount of fuel which would generate as much heat as its body if burned immediately after death". I do not know how he has found this out, but he is a man of science – how then can it be objected against the future vitality of the machines that they are, in their present infancy, at the beck and call of beings who are themselves incapable of originating mechanical energy?

'The main point, however, to be observed as affording cause for alarm, is, that whereas animals were formerly the only stomachs of the machines, there are now many which have stomachs of their own, and consume their food themselves. This is a great step towards their becoming, if not animate, yet something so near akin to it, as not to differ more widely from our own life than animals do from vegetables. And though man should remain, in some respects, the higher creature, is not this in accordance with the practice of nature, which allows superiority in some things to animals which have, on the whole, been long surpassed? Has she not allowed the ant and the bee to retain superiority over man in the organization of their communities and social arrangements, the bird in traversing the air, the fish in swimming, the horse in strength and fleetness, and the dog in self-sacrifice?

'It is said by some with whom I have conversed upon this subject, that the machines can never be developed into animate or quasi-animate existence, inasmuch as they have no reproductive system, nor seem ever likely to possess one. If this be taken to mean that they cannot marry, and that we are never likely to see a fertile union between two vapour-engines with the young ones playing about the door of the shed, however greatly we might desire to do so, I will readily grant it. But the objection is not a very profound one. No one expects that all the features of the now existing organizations will be absolutely repeated in an entirely new class of life. The reproductive system of animals differs widely from that of plants, but both are reproductive systems. Has nature exhausted her phases of this power?

T—E

'Surely if a machine is able to reproduce another machine systematically, we may say that it has a reproductive system. What is a reproductive system, if it be not a system for reproduction? And how few of the machines are there which have not been produced systematically by other machines? But it is man that makes them do so. Yes; but is it not insects that make many of the plants reproductive, and would not whole families of plants die out if their fertilization was not effected by a class of agents utterly foreign to themselves? Does anyone say that the red clover had no reproductive system because the humble bee (and the humble bee only) must aid and abet it before it can reproduce? No one. The humble bee is a part of the reproductive system of the clover. Each one of ourselves has sprung from minute animalcules whose entity was entirely distinct from our own, and which acted after their kind with no thought or heed of what we might think about it. These little creatures are part of our own reproductive system; then why not we part of that of the machines?

'But the machines which produce machinery do not produce machines after their own kind. A thimble may be made by machinery, but it is not made by, neither will it ever make, a thimble. Here, again, if we turn to nature we shall find abundance of analogies which will teach us that a reproductive system may be in full force without the thing produced being of the same kind as that which produced it. Very few creatures reproduce after their own kind; they reproduce something which has the potentiality of becoming that which their parents were. Thus the butterfly lays an egg, which egg can become a caterpillar, which caterpillar can become a chrysalis, which chrysalis can become a butterfly; and though I freely grant that the machines cannot be said to have more than the germ of a true reproductive system at present, have we not just seen that they have only recently obtained the germs of a mouth and stomach? And may not some stride be made in the direction of true reproduction which shall be as great as that which has been recently taken in the direction of true feeding?

'It is possible that the system when developed may be in many cases a vicarious thing. Certain classes of machines may be alone fertile, while the rest discharge other functions in the mechanical system, just as the great majority of ants and bees have nothing to do with the continuation of their species, but get food and store it, without thought of breeding. One cannot expect the parallel to be complete or nearly so; certainly not now, and probably never; but is there not enough analogy existing at the present moment, to make us feel seriously uneasy about the future, and to render it our duty to check the evil while we can still do so? Machines can within certain limits beget machines of any class, no matter how different to themselves. Every class of machines will probably have its special mechanical breeders, and all the higher ones will owe their existence to a large number of parents and not to two only.

'We are misled by considering any complicated machine as a single thing; in truth it is a city or society, each member of which was bred truly after its kind. We see a machine as a whole, we call it by a name and individualize it; we look at our own limbs, and know that the combination forms an individual which springs from a single centre of reproductive action; we therefore assume that there can be no reproductive action which does not arise from a single centre; but this assumption is unscientific, and the bare fact that no vapour-engine was ever made entirely by another, or two others, of its own kind, is not sufficient to warrant us as saying that vapour-engines have no reproductive system. The truth is that each part of every vapour-engine is bred by its own special breeders, whose function it is to breed that part, and that only, while the combination of the parts into a whole forms another department of the mechanical reproductive system, which is at present exceedingly complex and difficult to see in its entirety.

'Complex now, but how much simpler and more intelligibly organized may it not become in another hundred thousand years? Or in twenty thousand? For man at present believes that his interest lies in that direction; he spends an incalculable amount of labour and time and thought in making machines breed always better and better; he has already succeeded in effecting much that at one time appeared impossible, and there seem no limits to the results of accumulated improvements if they are allowed to descend with modification from generation to generation. It must always be remembered that man's body is what it is through having been moulded into its present shape by the changes of many millions of years, but that his organization never advanced with anything like the rapidity with which that of the machines is advancing. This is the most alarming feature in the case, and I must be pardoned for insisting on it so frequently. . . .

'If the above is sound, it follows that the regularity wit
which machinery acts is no proof of the absence of vitality, c
at least of germs which may be developed into a new phase c
life. At first sight it would indeed appear that a vapour-engin
cannot help going when set upon a line of rails with the steam u
and the machinery in full play; whereas the man whose busine
it is to drive it can help doing so at any moment that he please
so that the first has no spontaneity, and is not possessed of an
sort of free will, while the second has and is.

'This is true up to a certain point; the driver can stop th
engine at any moment that he pleases, but he can only please
do so at certain points which have been fixed for him by other
or in the case of unexpected obstructions which force him t
please to do so. His pleasure is not spontaneous; there is an ur
seen choir of influences around him, which make it impossib
for him to act in any other way than one. It is known beforehan
how much strength must be given to these influences, just as
is known beforehand how much coal and water are necessar
for the vapour-engine itself; and curiously enough it will t
found that the influences brought to bear upon the driver are c
the same kind as those brought to bear upon the engine – tha
is to say, food and warmth. The driver is obedient to his master
because he gets food and warmth from them, and if these a
withheld or given in insufficient quantities he will cease to driv
in like manner the engine will cease to work if it is insufficientl
fed. The only difference is, that the man is conscious about h
wants, and the engine (beyond refusing to work) does not seer
to be so; but this is temporary, and has been dealt with above.

'Accordingly, the requisite strength being given to the motive
that are to drive the driver, there has never, or hardly ever, bee
an instance of a man stopping his engine through wantonnes
But such a case might occur; yes, and it might occur that th
engine should break down; but if the train is stopped from som
trivial motive it will be found either that the strength of th
necessary influences has been miscalculated, or that the man ha
been miscalculated, in the same way as an engine may break dow
from an unsuspected flaw; but even in such a case there will hav
been no spontaneity; the action will have had its true parenta
causes; spontaneity is only a term for man's ignorance of the god

'Is there, then, no spontaneity on the part of those who driv
the driver?'

Here followed an obscure argument upon this subject, whic

I have thought it best to omit. The writer resumes: 'After all then it comes to this, that the difference between the life of a man and that of a machine is one rather of degree than of kind, though differences in kind are not wanting. An animal has more provision for emergency than a machine. The machine is less versatile; its range of action is narrow; its strength and accuracy in its own sphere are superhuman, but it shows badly in a dilemma; sometimes when its normal action is disturbed, it will lose its head, and go from bad to worse like a lunatic in a raging frenzy; but here, again, we are met by the same consideration as before, namely, that the machines are still in their infancy; they are mere skeletons without muscles and flesh.

'For how many emergencies is an oyster adapted? For as many as are likely to happen to it, and no more. So are the machines; and so is man himself. The list of casualties that daily occur to man through his want of adaptability is probably as great as that occurring to the machines; and every day gives them some greater provision for the unforeseen. Let anyone examine the wonderful self-regulating and self-adjusting contrivances which are now incorporated with the vapour-engine, let him watch the way in which it supplies itself with oil; in which it indicates its wants to those who tend it; in which, by the governor, it regulates its application of its own strength; let him look at that store-house of inertia and momentum the fly-wheel, or at the buffers on a railway carriage; let him see how those improvements are being selected for perpetuity which contain provision against the emergencies that may arise to harass the machines, and then let him think of a hundred thousand years, and the accumulated progress which they will bring unless man can be awakened to a sense of his situation, and of the doom which he is preparing for himself.*

* Since my return to England, I have been told that those who are conversant about machines use many terms concerning them which show that their vitality is here recognized, and that a collection of expressions in use among those who attend on steam engines would be no less startling than instructive. I am also informed, that almost all machines have their own tricks and idiosyncrasies; that they know their drivers and keepers; and that they will play pranks upon a stranger. It is my intention, on a future occasion, to bring together examples both of the expression in common use among mechanicians, and of any extraordinary exhibitions of mechanical sagacity and eccentricity that I can meet with – not as believing in the Erewhonian Professor's theory, but from the interest of the subject.

'The misery is that man has been blind so long already. In his reliance upon the use of steam he has been betrayed into increasing and multiplying. To withdraw steam power suddenly will not have the effect of reducing us to the state in which we were before its introduction; there will be a general break-up and time of anarchy such as has never been known; it will be as though our population were suddenly doubled, with no additional means of feeding the increased number. The air we breathe is hardly more necessary for our animal life than the use of any machine, on the strength of which we have increased our numbers, is to our civilization; it is the machines which act upon man and make him man, as much as man who has acted upon and made the machines; but we must choose between the alternative of undergoing much present suffering, or seeing ourselves gradually superseded by our own creatures, till we rank no higher in comparison with them, than the beasts of the field with ourselves.

'Herein lies our danger. For many seem inclined to acquiesce in so dishonourable a future. They say that although man should become to the machines what the horse and dog are to us, yet that he will continue to exist, and will probably be better off in a state of domestication under the beneficent rule of the machines than in his present wild condition. We treat our domestic animals with much kindness. We give them whatever we believe to be the best for them; and there can be no doubt that our use of meat has increased their happiness rather than detracted from it. In like manner there is reason to hope that the machines will use us kindly, for their existence will be in a great measure dependent upon ours; they will rule us with a rod of iron, but they will not eat us; they will not only require our services in the reproduction and education of their young, but also in waiting upon them as servants; in gathering food for them, and feeding them; in restoring them to health when they are sick; and in either burying their dead or working up their deceased members into new forms of mechanical existence.

'The very nature of the motive power which works the advancement of the machines precludes the possibility of man's life being rendered miserable as well as enslaved. Slaves are tolerably happy if they have good masters, and the revolution will not occur in our time, nor hardly in ten thousand years, or ten times that. Is it wise to be uneasy about a contingency which is so remote? Man is not a sentimental animal where his material interests are concerned, and though here and there some ardent soul may look upon himself and curse his fate that he was not born a vapour-engine, yet the mass of mankind will acquiesce in any arrangement which gives them better food and clothing at a cheaper rate, and will refrain from yielding to unreasonable jealousy merely because there are other destinies more glorious than their own.

'The power of custom is enormous, and so gradual will be the change, that man's sense of what is due to himself will be at no time rudely shocked; our bondage will steal upon us noiselessly and by imperceptible approaches; nor will there ever be such a clashing of desires between man and the machines as will lead to an encounter between them. Among themselves the machines will war eternally, but they will still require man as the being through whose agency the struggle will be principally conducted. In point of fact there is no occasion for anxiety about the future happiness of man so long as he continues to be in any way profitable to the machines; he may become the inferior race, but he will be infinitely better off than he is now. Is it not then both absurd and unreasonable to be envious of our benefactors? And should we not be guilty of consummate folly if we were to reject advantages which we cannot obtain otherwise, merely because they involve a greater gain to others than to ourselves?

'With those who can argue in this way I have nothing in common. I shrink with as much horror from believing that my race can ever be superseded or surpassed, as I should do from believing that even at the remotest period my ancestors were other than human beings. Could I believe that ten hundred thousand years ago a single one of my ancestors was another kind of being to myself, I should lose all self-respect, and take no further pleasure or interest in life. I have the same feeling with regard to my descendants, and believe it to be one that will be felt so generally that the country will resolve upon putting an immediate stop to all further mechanical progress, and upon destroying all improvements that have been made for the last three hundred years. I would not urge more than this. We may trust ourselves to deal with those that remain, and though I should prefer to have seen the destruction include another two hundred years, I am aware of the necessity for compromising, and would so far sacrifice my own individual convictions as to be content with three hundred. Less than this will be insufficient.'

THE CONQUEST OF THE AIR

EDGAR ALLAN POE

The Balloon Hoax

It is hard to imagine in these times that within living memory the idea of what used to be called a 'flying machine' was generally regarded as preposterous, so that any story of a successful flight by, say, an aeroplane or a helicopter, would at once have been classed as science fiction. In spite of a few short flights by rather clumsy dirigible balloons, the idea of a long-distance being achieved by such a contrivance would have been similarly regarded throughout much of the nineteenth century.

Edgar Allan Poe (1809–1849) owes much of his fame to his 'horror stories', but he was also a poet, a literary critic, the founder of the analytical detective story, and a pioneer of science fiction. He wrote an 'end of the world' story, an absurd moon travel story, revealed by its ending to be another hoax, and an unfinished story, afterwards 'completed' by Jules Verne,* of fantastic adventures in the Far South.

Though he only trifled with science fiction, he contributed to this novel art form one of its chief features, that sober matter-of-fact style which Jules Verne and his successors have used to such good effect, and which enabled *The Balloon Hoax* to impose for a time on the public credulity.

THE BALLOON HOAX

(Astounding News by Express, *viâ* Norfolk! – The Atlantic Crossed in Three Days! Signal Triumph of Mr. Monck Mason's Flying Machine! – Arrival at Sullivan's Island, near Charleston, S.C., of Mr. Mason, Mr. Robert Holland, Mr. Henson, Mr. Harrison Ainsworth, and four others, in the Steering Balloon,

* *The Mystery of Arthur Gordon Pym*, by Edgar Allan Poe and Jules Verne, published by Panther Books.

Victoria, after a passage of Seventy-five hours from Land to Land! Full Particulars of the Voyage!

The subjoined *jeu d'esprit* with the preceding heading in magnificent capitals, well interspersed with notes of admiration, was originally published, as matter of fact, in the *New York Sun,* a daily newspaper, and therein fully subserved the purpose of creating indigestible aliment for the *quidnuncs* during the few hours intervening between a couple of the Charleston mails. The rush for the 'sole paper which had the news', was something beyond even the prodigious; and, in fact, if (as some assert) the *Victoria* did not absolutely accomplish the voyage recorded, it will be difficult to assign a reason why she *should* not have accomplished it.)

The great problem is at length solved! The air, as well as the earth and the ocean, has been subdued by science, and will become a common and convenient highway for mankind. *The Atlantic has been actually crossed in a Balloon!* and this too without difficulty – without any great apparent danger – with thorough control of the machine – and in the inconceivably brief period of seventy-five hours from shore to shore! By the energy of an agent at Charleston, S.C., we are enabled to be the first to furnish the public with a detailed account of this most extraordinary voyage, which was performed between Saturday, the 6th instant, at 11 a.m., and 2 p.m., on Tuesday, the 9th instant, by Sir Everard Bringhurst; Mr. Osborne, a nephew of Lord Bentinck's; Mr. Monck Mason and Mr. Robert Holland, the well-known aëronauts; Mr. Harrison Ainsworth, author of *Jack Shepherd,* etc.; and Mr. Henson, the projector of the late unsuccessful flying machine – with two seamen from Woolwich – in all, eight persons. The particulars furnished below may be relied on as authentic and accurate in every respect, as, with a slight exception, they are copied *verbatim* from the joint diaries of Mr. Monck Mason and Mr. Harrison Ainsworth, to whose politeness our agent is indebted for much verbal information respecting the balloon itself, its construction, and other matters of interest. The only alteration in the MS received, has been made for the purpose of throwing the hurried account of our agent, Mr. Forsyth, into a connected and intelligible form.

THE BALLOON

'Two very decided failures, of late, – those of Mr. Henson and

Sir George Cayley – had much weakened the public interest in the subject of aërial navigation. Mr. Henson's scheme (which at first was considered very feasible even by men of science) was founded upon the principle of an inclined plane, started from an eminence by an extrinsic force applied and continued by the revolution of impinging vanes in form and number resembling the vanes of a windmill. But, in all the experiments made with models at the Adelaide Gallery, it was found that the operation of these fans not only did not propel the machine, but actually impeded its flight. The only propelling force it ever exhibited, was the mere *impetus* acquired from the descent of the inclined plane; and this *impetus* carried the machine farther when the vanes were at rest, than when they were in motion – a fact which sufficiently demonstrated their inutility; and in the absence of the propelling, which was also the *sustaining*, power the whole fabric would necessarily descend. This consideration led Sir George Cayley to think only of adapting a propeller to some machine having of itself an independent power of support – in a word, to a balloon; the idea however, being novel, or original, with Sir George, only so far as regards the mode of its application to practice. He exhibited a model of his invention at the Polytechnic Institution. The propelling principle, or power was here, also, applied to interrupted surfaces, or vanes, put in revolution. These vanes were four in number, but were found entirely ineffectual in moving the balloon, or in aiding its ascending power. The whole project was thus a complete failure.

'It was at this juncture that Mr. Monck Mason (whose voyage from Dover to Weilburg in the balloon, *Nassau*, occasioned so much excitement in 1837) conceived the idea of employing the principle of the Archimedean screw for the purpose of propulsion through the air – rightly attributing the failure of Mr Henson's scheme, and of Sir George Cayley's to the interruption of surface in the independent vanes. He made the first public experiment at Willis's Rooms, but afterward removed his model to the Adelaide Gallery.

'Like Sir George Cayley's balloon, his own was an ellipsoid Its length was thirteen feet six inches – height, six feet eight inches. It contained about three hundred and twenty cubic feet of gas, which, if pure hydrogen, would support twenty-one pounds upon its first inflation, before the gas has time to deteriorate or escape. The weight of the whole machine and apparatus was seventeen pounds – leaving about four pounds to spare. Beneath the centre of the balloon, was a frame of light wood, about nine feet long, and rigged on to the balloon itself with a network in the customary manner. From this framework was suspended a wicker basket or car.

'The screw consists of an axis of hollow brass tube, eighteen inches in length, through which, upon a semispiral inclined at fifteen degrees, pass a series of steel-wire radii, two feet long, and thus projecting a foot on either side. These radii are connected at the outer extremities by two bands of flattened wire – the whole in this manner forming the framework of the screw, which is completed by a covering of oiled silk cut into gores, and tightened so as to present a tolerably uniform surface. At each end of its axis this screw is supported by pillars of hollow brass tube descending from the hoop. In the lower ends of these tubes are holes in which the pivots of the axis revolve. From the end of the axis which is next the car, proceeds a shaft of steel, connecting the screw with the pinion of a piece of spring machinery fixed in the car. By the operation of this spring, the screw is made to revolve with great rapidity, communicating a progressive motion to the whole. By means of the rudder, the machine was readily turned in any direction. The spring was of great power, compared with its dimensions, being capable of raising forty-five pounds upon a barrel of four inches diameter after the first turn, and gradually increasing as it was wound up. It weighed, altogether, eight pounds six ounces. The rudder was a light frame of cane covered with silk, shaped somewhat like a battledore, and was about three feet long, and at the widest, one foot. Its weight was about two ounces. It could be turned *flat,* and directed upward or downward, as well as to the right or left; and thus enabled the aëronaut to transfer the resistance of the air which in an inclined position it must generate in its passage, to any side upon which he might desire to act; thus determining the balloon in the opposite direction.

'This model (which, through want of time, we have necessarily described in an imperfect manner) was put in action at the Adelaide Gallery, where it accomplished a velocity of five miles per hour; although, strange to say, it excited very little interest in comparison with the previous complex machine of Mr. Henson – so resolute is the world to despise anything which carries with it an air of simplicity. To accomplish the great desideratum of aërial navigation, it was generally supposed that some

exceedingly complicated application must be made of some unusually profound principle in dynamics.

'So well satisfied, however, was Mr. Mason of the ultimate
success of his invention, that he determined to construct immediately, if possible, a balloon of sufficient capacity to test the question by a voyage of some extent – the original design being to
cross the British Channel, as before, in the *Nassau* balloon. To
carry out his views, he solicited and obtained the patronage of
Sir Everard Bringhurst and Mr. Osborne, two gentlemen well
known for scientific acquirement, and especially for the interest
they have exhibited in the progress of aërostation. The project,
at the desire of Mr. Osborne, was kept a profound secret from
the public – the only persons entrusted with the design being
those actually engaged in the construction of the machine, which
was built (under the superintendence of Mr. Mason, Mr. Holland, Sir Everard Bringhurst, and Mr. Osborne) at the seat
of the latter gentleman near Penstruthal, in Wales. Mr. Henson,
accompanied by his friend Mr. Ainsworth, was admitted to
a private view of the balloon, on Saturday last – when the
two gentlemen made final arrangements to be included in
the adventure. We are not informed for what reason the
two seamen were also included in the party – but in the
course of a day or two, we shall put our readers in possession
of the minutest particulars respecting this extraordinary
voyage.

'The balloon is composed of silk, varnished with the liquid
gum caoutchouc. It is of vast dimensions, containing more than
40,000 cubic feet of gas; but as coal-gas was employed in place
of the more expensive and inconvenient hydrogen, the supporting power of the machine, when fully inflated, and immediately
after inflation, is not more than about 2500 pounds. The coal-
gas is not only much less costly, but is easily procured and managed.

'For its introduction into common use for purposes of aërostation, we are indebted to Mr. Charles Green. Up to his discovery, the process of inflation was not only exceedingly expensive, but uncertain. Two and even three days have frequently
been wasted in futile attempts to procure a sufficiency of hydrogen to fill a balloon, from which it had great tendency to escape
owing to its extreme subtlety, and its affinity for the surrounding
atmosphere. In a balloon sufficiently perfect to retain its content
of coal-gas unaltered, in quality or amount, for six months, a

equal quantity of hydrogen could not be maintained in equal purity for six weeks.

'The supporting power being estimated at 2500 pounds, and the united weights of the party amounting only to about 1200, there was left a surplus of 1300, of which again 1200 was exhausted by ballast, arranged in bags of different sizes, with their respective weights marked upon them – by cordage, barometers, telescopes, barrels containing provision for a fortnight, watercasks, cloaks, carpet-bags, and various other indispensable matters, including a coffee-warmer, contrived for warming coffee by means of slack-lime, so as to dispense altogether with fire, if it should be judged prudent to do so. All these articles, with the exception of the ballast, and a few trifles, were suspended from the hoop overhead. The car is much smaller and lighter, in proportion, than the one appended to the model. It is formed of a light wicker, and is wonderfully strong, for so frail-looking a machine. Its rim is about four feet deep. The rudder is also very much larger, in proportion, than that of the model; and the screw is considerably smaller. The balloon is furnished besides with a grapnel, and a guide-rope; which latter is of the most indispensable importance. A few words, in explanation, will here be necessary for such of our readers as are not conversant with the details of aërostation.

'As soon as the balloon quits the earth, it is subjected to the influence of many circumstances tending to create a difference in its weight; augmenting or diminishing its ascending power. For example, there may be a deposition of dew upon the silk, to the extent, even of several hundred pounds; ballast has then to be thrown out, or the machine may descend. This ballast being discarded, and a clear sunshine evaporating the dew, and at the same time expanding the gas in the silk, the whole will again rapidly ascend. To check this ascent, the only resource is (or rather was, until Mr. Green's invention of the guide-rope) the permission of the escape of gas from the valve; but, in the loss of gas, is a proportionate general loss of ascending power; so that, in a comparatively brief period, the best-constructed balloon must necessarily exhaust all its resources, and come to the earth. This was the great obstacle to voyages of length.

'The guide-rope remedies the difficulty in the simplest manner conceivable. It is merely a very long rope which is suffered to trail from the car, and the effect of which is to prevent the balloon from changing its level in any material degree. If, for example, there should be a deposition of moisture upon the silk, and the machine begins to descend in consequence, there will be no necessity for discharging ballast to remedy the increase of weight, for it is remedied, or counteracted in an exactly just proportion, by the deposit on the ground of just so much of the end of the rope as is necessary. If, on the other hand, any circumstances should cause undue levity, and consequent ascent, this levity is immediately counteracted by the additional weight of rope upraised from the earth. Thus, the balloon can neither ascend nor descend, except within very narrow limits, and its resources, either in gas or ballast, remain comparatively unimpaired. When passing over an expanse of water, it becomes necessary to employ kegs of copper or wood, filled with liquid ballast of a lighter nature than water. These float, and serve all the purposes of a mere rope on land. Another most important office of the guide-rope, is to point out the *direction* of the balloon. The rope *drags*, either on land or sea, while the balloon is free; the latter, consequently, is always in advance, when any progress whatever is made: a comparison, therefore, by means of the compass, of the relative positions of the two objects, will always indicate the *course*. In the same way, the angle formed by the rope with the verticle axis of the machine, indicates the *velocity*. When there is no angle — in other words, when the rope hangs perpendicularly, the whole apparatus is stationary; but the larger the angle, that is to say, the farther the balloon precedes the end of the rope, the greater the velocity; and the converse.

'As the original design was to cross the British Channel, and alight as near Paris as possible, the voyagers had taken the precaution to prepare themselves with passports directed to all parts of the Continent, specifying the nature of the expedition, as in the case of the *Nassau* voyage, and entitling the adventurers to exemption from the usual formalities of office; unexpected events, however, rendered these passports superfluous.

'The inflation was commenced very quietly at daybreak, on Saturday morning, the 6th instant, in the courtyard of Weal-Vor House, Mr. Osborne's seat, about a mile from Penstruthal, in North Wales; and at seven minutes past eleven, everything being ready for departure, the balloon was set free, rising gently but steadily, in a direction nearly south; no use being made, for the first half hour, of either the screw or the rudder. We proceed now with the journal, as transcribed by Mr. Forsyth from the joint MSS. of Mr. Monck Mason and Mr. Ainsworth. The body of the journal, as given, is in the handwriting of Mr. Mason, and a P.S. is appended, each day, by Mr. Ainsworth, who has in preparation, and will shortly give the public a more minute and, no doubt, a thrillingly interesting account of the voyage.

THE JOURNAL

'*Saturday, April the 6th.* – Every preparation likely to embarrass us having been made overnight, we commenced the inflation this morning at daybreak; but owing to a thick fog, which encumbered the folds of the silk and rendered it unmanageable, we did not get through before nearly eleven o'clock. Cut loose, then, in high spirits, and rose gently but steadily, with a light breeze at north, which bore us in the direction of the Bristol Channel. Found the ascending force greater than we had expected; and as we arose higher and so got clear of the cliffs, and more in the sun's rays, our ascent became very rapid. I did not wish, however, to lose gas at so early a period of the adventure, and so concluded to ascend for the present. We soon ran out our guide-rope; but even when we had raised it clear of the earth, we still went up very rapidly. The balloon was unusually steady, and looked beautifully. In about ten minutes after starting, the barometer indicated an altitude of 15,000 feet. The weather was remarkably fine, and the view of the subjacent country – a most romantic one when seen from any point – was now especially sublime. The numerous deep gorges presented the appearance of lakes, on account of the dense vapour with which they were filled, and the pinnacles and crags to the south-east, piled in inextricable confusion resembling nothing so much as the giant cities of Eastern fable. We were rapidly approaching the mountains in the south, but our elevation was more than sufficient to enable us to pass them in safety. In a few minutes we soared over them in fine style; and Mr. Ainsworth, with the seamen, was surprised at their apparent want of altitude when viewed from the car, the tendency of great elevation in a balloon being to reduce inequalities of the surface below, to nearly a dead level. At half-past eleven still proceeding nearly south, we obtained our first view of the Bristol Channel; and, in fifteen minutes afterward, the line of breakers on the coast appeared immediately beneath us, and we were fairly out at sea. We now resolved to let off enough gas to bring our guide-rope, with the buoys affixed, into the water. This was immediately done, and we commenced a gradual descent. In about twenty minutes our first buoy dipped, and at the touch of the second soon afterward, we remained stationary as to elevation. We were all now anxious to test the efficiency of the rudder and screw, and we put them both into requisition forthwith, for the purpose of altering our direction more to the eastward, and in a line for Paris. By means of the rudder we instantly effected the necessary change of direction, and our course was brought nearly at right angles to that of the wind; when we set in motion the spring of the screw, and were rejoiced to find it propel as readily as desired. Upon this we gave nine hearty cheers, and dropped in the sea a bottle, inclosing a slip of parchment with a brief account of the principle of the invention. Hardly, however, had we done with our rejoicings, when an unforeseen accident occurred which discouraged us in no little degree. The steel rod connecting the spring with the propeller was suddenly jerked out of place, at the car end (by a swaying of the car through some movement of one of the two seamen we had taken up), and in an instant hung dangling out of reach, from the pivot of the axis of the screw. While we were endeavouring to regain it, our attention being completely absorbed, we became involved in a strong current of wind from the east, which bore us, with rapidly increasing force, toward the Atlantic. We soon found ourselves driving out to sea at the rate of not less, certainly, than fifty or sixty miles an hour, so that we came up with Cape Clear, at some forty miles to our north, before we had secured the rod, and had time to think what we were about. It was now that Mr. Ainsworth made an extraordinary but, to my fancy, a by no means unreasonable or chimerical proposition, in which he was instantly seconded by Mr. Holland – viz.: that we should take advantage of the strong gale which bore us on, and in place of beating back to Paris, make an attempt to reach the coast of North America. After slight reflection I gave a willing assent to this bold proposition, which (strange to say) met with objection from the two seamen only. As the stronger party, however, we overruled their fears, and kept resolutely upon our course. We steered due west; but as the trailing of the buoys materially impeded our progress, and we had the balloon abundantly at command, either for ascent or descent, we first threw out fifty pounds of ballast, and then

wound up (by means of the windlass) so much of the rope as
brought it quite clear of the sea. We perceived the effect of this
manoeuvre immediately, in a vastly increased rate of progress;
and, as the gale freshened, we flew with a velocity nearly inconceivable; the guide-rope flying out behind the car, like a streamer
from a vessel. It is needless to say that a very short time sufficed
us to lose sight of the coast. We passed over innumerable vessels
of all kinds, a few of which were endeavouring to beat up,
but the most of them lying to. We occasioned the greatest excitement on board all – an excitement greatly relished by ourselves,
and especially by our two men, who, now under the influence of
a dram of Geneva, seemed resolved to give all scruple, or fear,
to the wind. Many of the vessels fired signal guns; and in all
we were saluted with loud cheers (which we heard with surprising distinctness) and the waving of caps and handkerchiefs. We
kept on in this manner throughout the day with no material
incident, and, as the shades of night closed around us, we made a
rough estimate of the distance traversed. It could not have been
less than five hundred miles, and was probably much more. The
propeller was kept in constant operation, and, no doubt, aided
our progress materially. As the sun went down, the gale freshened into an absolute hurricane, and the ocean beneath was
clearly visible on account of its phosphorescence. The wind was
from the east all night, and gave us the brightest omen of success. We suffered no little from cold, and the dampness of the
atmosphere was most unpleasant; but the ample space in the car
enabled us to lie down, and by means of cloaks and a few blan-
kets we did sufficiently well.

'P.S. [by Mr. Ainsworth.] The last nine hours have been unquestionably the most exciting of my life. I can conceive nothing
more sublimating than the strange peril and novelty of an adventure such as this. May God grant that we succeed! I ask not
success for mere safety to my insignificant person, but for the
sake of human knowledge and – for the vastness of the triumph.
And yet the feat is only so evidently feasible that the sole wonder
is why men have scrupled to attempt it before. One single gale
such as now befriends us – let such a tempest whirl forward a
balloon for four or five days (these gales often last longer) and
the voyager will be easily borne, in that period, from coast to
coast. In view of such a gale the broad Atlantic becomes a mere
lake. I am more struck, just now, with the supreme silence which
reigns in the sea beneath us, notwithstanding its agitation, than

with any other phenomenon presenting itself. The waters giv
up no voice to the heavens. The immense flaming ocean writhe
and is tortured uncomplainingly. The mountainous surge
suggest the idea of innumerable dumb gigantic fiends strug
gling in impotent agony. In a night such as is this to me, a mai
lives – lives a whole century of ordinary life – nor would I forg
this rapturous delight for that of a whole century of ordinary
existence.

'*Sunday, the 7th*. [*Mr. Mason's MS.*] This morning the gale
by then, had subsided to an eight- or nine-knot breeze (for a vesse
at sea), and bears us, perhaps, thirty miles per hour, or more. I
has veered, however, very considerably to the north; and now
at sundown, we are holding our course due west, principall
by the screw and rudder, which answer their purposes to admira
tion. I regard the project as thoroughly successful, and the easy
navigation of the air in any direction (not exactly in the teet
of a gale) as no longer problematical. We could not have mad
head against the strong wind of yesterday; but, by ascending, w
might have got out of its influence, if requisite. Against a pretty
stiff breeze, I feel convinced, we can make our way with the pro
peller. At noon, today, ascended to an elevation of nearly 25,00
feet, by discharging ballast. Did this to search for a more direc
current, but found none so favourable as the one we are now in
We have an abundance of gas to take us across this small pond
even should the voyage last three weeks. I have not the slightes
fear for the result. The difficulty has been strangely exaggerate
and misapprehended. I can choose my current, and should
find *all* currents against me, I can make very tolerable headway
with the propeller. We have had no incidents worth recording
The night promises fair.

'P.S. [By Mr. Ainsworth.] I have little to record, except th
fact (to me quite a surprising one) that, at an elevation equa
to that of Cotopaxi, I experienced neither very intense cold no
headache, nor difficulty of breathing; neither, I find, did Mr
Mason, nor Mr. Holland, nor Sir Everard. Mr. Osborne com
plained of constriction of the chest – but this soon wore off
We have flown at a great rate during the day, and we must be
more than half way across the Atlantic. We have passed over
some twenty or thirty vessels of various kinds, and all seem to
be delightfully astonished. Crossing the ocean in a balloon i
not so difficult a feat after all. *Omne ignotum pro magnifico*
Mem.: at 25,000 feet elevation the sky appears nearly black, and

the stars are distinctly visible; while the sea does not seem convex (as one might suppose) but absolutely and most unequivocally concave.*

'*Monday, the 8th.* [*Mr. Mason's MS.*] This morning we had again some little trouble with the rod of the propeller, which must be entirely remodelled, for fear of serious accident – I mean the steel rod, not the vanes. The latter could not be improved. The wind has been blowing steadily and strongly from the north-east all day; and so far fortune seems bent upon favouring us. Just before day, we were all somewhat alarmed at some odd noises and concussions in the balloon, accompanied with the apparent rapid subsidence of the whole machine. These phenomena were occasioned by the expansion of the gas, through increase of heat in the atmosphere, and the consequent disruption of the minute particles of ice with which the net-work had become encrusted during the night. Threw down several bottles to the vessels below. See one of them picked up by a large ship – seemingly one of the New York line packets. Endeavoured to make out her name, but could not be sure of it. Mr. Osborne's telescope made it out something like *Atalanta*. It is now twelve at night, and we are still going nearly west, at a rapid pace. The sea is peculiarly phosphorescent.

'P.S. [By Mr. Ainsworth.] It is now two A.M., and nearly calm, as well as I can judge – but it is very difficult to determine this point, since we move with the air so completely. I have not

* NOTE.—Mr. Ainsworth has not attempted to account for this phenomenon, which, however, is quite susceptible of explanation. A line dropped from an elevation of 25,000 feet, perpendicularly to the surface of the earth (or sea), would form the perpendicular of a right-angled triangle, of which the base would extend from the right angle to the horizon, and the hypothenuse from the horizon to the balloon. But the 25,000 feet of altitude is little or nothing, in comparison with the extent of the prospect. In other words, the base and hypothenuse of the supposed triangle would be so long, when compared with the perpendicular, that the two former may be regarded as nearly parallel. In this manner the horizon of the aëronaut would appear to be *on a level* with the car. But, as the point immediately beneath him seems, and is, at a great distance below him, it seems, of course, also, at a great distance below the horizon. Hence the impression of *concavity*; and this impression must remain, until the elevation shall bear so great a proportion to the extent of prospect, that the apparent parallelism of the base and hypothenuse disappears – when the earth's real convexity must become apparent.

slept since quitting Weal-Vor, but can stand it no longer, and must take a nap. We cannot be far from the American coast.

'*Tuesday, the 9th.* [*Mr. Ainsworth's MS.*] One P.M. *We are in full view of the low coast of South Carolina.* The great problem is accomplished. We have crossed the Atlantic – fairly and easily crossed it in a balloon! God be praised! Who shall say that anything is impossible hereafter?'

The Journal here ceases. Some particulars of the descent were communicated, however, by Mr. Ainsworth to Mr. Forsyth. It was nearly dead calm when the voyagers first came in view of the coast, which was immediately recognized by both the seamen, and by Mr. Osborne. The latter gentleman having acquaintances at Fort Moultrie, it was immediately resolved to descend in its vicinity. The balloon was brought over the beach (the tide being out and the sand hard, smooth, and admirably adapted for a descent), and the grapnel let go, which took firm hold at once. The inhabitants of the island, and of the fort, thronged out, of course, to see the balloon; but it was with the greatest difficulty that any one could be made to credit the actual voyage – *the crossing of the Atlantic.* The grapnel caught at two P.M. precisely; and thus the whole voyage was completed in seventy-five hours; or rather less, counting from shore to shore. No serious accident occurred. No real danger was at any time apprehended. The balloon was exhausted and secured without trouble; and when the MS. from which this narrative is compiled was despatched from Charleston, the party were still at Fort Moultrie. Their further intentions were not ascertained; but we can safely promise our readers some additional information either on Monday or in the course of the next day, at furthest.

This is unquestionably the most stupendous, the most interesting, and the most important undertaking ever accomplished or even attempted by man. What magnificent events may ensue it would be useless now to think of determining.

INTO THE UNKNOWN

JULES VERNE

from *Twenty Thousand Leagues under the Sea*

Jules Verne (1828–1905) may reasonably be regarded as the founder of modern science fiction. Though he was much influenced by the work of Edgar Allan Poe, whom he greatly admired, he fully realized that author's limitations. He took science fiction, which Poe had only played with, quite seriously and devoted much of his life to its systematic development. Scorning to deflate his stories, as his forerunner had done, with hoaxes, he converted them into the legitimate literary device in which he delighted, the Vernian 'surprise ending'.

After years of disappointment he suddenly leaped into fame with the first of his 'Strange Journeys', *Five Weeks in a Balloon* (1863), and he followed this up with a series of adventure stories whose theme was the exploration of the unknown.

Rather a geographer than a story-teller, he adopted the fictional form largely because it was the best way of conveying the information which so much fascinated him: he took his heroes across 'Darkest Africa', into the earth's interior, to the North Pole, round the world, and into outer space. It seemed only natural that he should make the next of his 'Strange Journeys' a voyage into the ocean depths.

A factual basis for his narrative was, so to speak, ready to hand: it was not so very long before that a pioneer submarine had been sunk, and somewhat earlier another, that constructed in 1800 by Robert Fulton, has made a successful cruise. Here was even a name for the super-submarine which he had in mind, for Fulton's vessel had been called the *Nautilus*.

For boldness of conception, descriptive brilliance, and strong characterization, *Twenty Thousand Leagues under the Sea* (1870) is generally regarded as Jules Verne's masterpiece. It owes much of its force to its author's love of the sea: in his boyhood Verne had aspired to become a ship's captain and had actually 'run away to sea', though only to be brought home in disgrace; and until he was crippled by a madman's bullet he had been an enthusiastic amateur yachtsman.

Loving freedom as much as he loved the sea, he made Captain Nemo, master of the *Nautilus*, a romantic exile, seeking refuge from society beneath the waters and deriving his food, his clothing, and even his cigars, from the creatures that live in their depths. He also made him an inventor not only of his submarine but of the self-contained diving-dresses which enable long excursions to be made across the sea-floor.

Verne, however, was fully aware of the legitimate claims that society made upon him, and sought to answer them by imparting information to the world. He therefore made the story's narrator, Professor Aronnax, a famous naturalist, delighted because his cruise in the *Nautilus* enabled him to study marine biology as no other savant had ever done but anxious to escape so as to give the result of his studies to the world. For in the story Captain Nemo, after rescuing Aronnax and two of his companions from drowning, had refused point-blank to let them return to civilization; he treats the Professor partly as a captive, and partly as an honoured guest.

THAT night, about eleven o'clock, I received a most unexpected visit from Captain Nemo.

'M. Aronnax, so far you have only visited the ocean depths by daylight. Would you care to see them in the darkness of the night?'

'Most willingly.'

'I warn you, the way will be tiring. We shall have far to walk and we must climb a mountain. The roads are not in good condition.'

'What you say, Captain, only heightens my curiosity; I'm ready to follow.'

In a few moments we had put on our diving-dresses, but no electric lamps were ready: 'They would be useless,' the captain assured me. Some minutes later we set foot on the bottom of the Atlantic at a depth of 150 fathoms. Midnight was near. The waters were profoundly dark, but Captain Nemo pointed out a reddish glare about two miles away. What this fire might be, what could feed it, why and how it lit up the water, I could not say.

As we advanced I heard a pattering above my head and I soon

understood its cause. It was rain falling violently on the waves. Instinctively the thought flashed across my mind that I should be wet through! By the water! In the water! I could not help laughing. But, indeed, in the thick diving-dress the liquid could no longer be felt, and we only seemed to be in an atmosphere somewhat denser than the air. Nothing more.

After half an hour's walk the ground became stony. Microscopic animals lit it up slightly with their phosphorescent gleam. My feet often slipped upon the sticky carpet of seaweed and without my iron-tipped stick I should have fallen more than once. Turning round, I could still see the light of the *Nautilus* beginning to pale in the distance.

But the rosy light which guided us increased. This fire below the water puzzled me greatly. Was it due to something unknown to earthly science? Or was it due to some human agency? Was I to meet in these depths friends of Captain Nemo whom he was going to visit, and who, like himself, led this strange existence? A whole colony of exiles who, weary of the miseries of earth, had sought and found independence in the deep? These foolish and unreasonable ideas pursued me, and I should not have been surprised to meet on the sea-floor one of those submarine towns of which the captain dreamed.

Our road became more and more brightly lit. The white glimmer came from the summit of a mountain about 800 feet high. But what I saw was simply a reflection produced by the clearness of the waters. The source of this light was a fire on the far side of the mountain.

Captain Nemo advanced without hesitation. He knew this dreary road. Doubtless he had often travelled over it and could not get lost. I followed him with unshaken confidence. He seemed like a genie of the sea, and I could not help admiring his figure, outlined in black against the gleam.

It was one in the morning when we arrived at the mountain; but first we had to venture through the difficult paths of a vast copse.

Yes; a copse of dead trees, without leaves, without sap, trees petrified by the action of the water and here and there overtopped by gigantic pines. It was like a pit in the coal measures, but with the trees that had formed them still standing. Imagine a forest on the sides of the mountain, but a forest swallowed up. The paths were encumbered with seaweed in which there grovelled a whole world of crustacea.

I went on, climbing over the rocks, striding over the tree trunks, breaking the sea-bindweed which hung from one tree to the other; and frightening the fishes, which flew from branch to branch. Pressing onward I felt no fatigue; I followed my guide who never tired.

What a spectacle! How can I express it? How paint the aspect of those woods and rocks – their lower parts dark and wild, their upper surfaces tinted red by that light which the water reflected? We climbed rocks which fell down behind us with the low growling of an avalanche. To right and left ran long, dark galleries, where the hand of man seemed to have worked, and I wondered if some inhabitant of these submarine regions would not suddenly appear before us.

But Captain Nemo was still climbing. I could not lag behind. A false step would have been dangerous, but I walked with a firm tread, not feeling any giddiness. Now I jumped a crevice whose depth would have made me hesitate on land; now I ventured on the unsteady trunk of a tree thrown across an abyss, without looking downwards, having eyes only to admire the desolation around me.

There were monumental rocks which seemed to defy all laws of equilibrium. From between their stony buttresses sprang trees, like jets of water under heavy pressure, natural towers, large scarps, cut perpendicularly, or inclined at an angle which the laws of gravitation could never have tolerated on land.

A hundred feet above our heads rose the mountain-top. Some petrified shrubs ran fantastically here and there. Fishes rose from under our feet like birds from the long grass. The massive rocks were rent with impenetrable fractures, deep caverns and unfathomable gulfs, in the depths of which formidable creatures might be heard moving. My blood curdled when I saw enormous antennae blocking my road or some frightful claw closing noisily in the shadow of the crannies. Millions of luminous points gleamed brightly in the midst of the darkness. They were the eyes of gigantic crustacea crouched in their holes; of giant lobsters, erect like halberdiers and waving their claws with a metallic clicking; of titanic crabs, pointed like a gun on its carriage, and of frightful squids, interweaving their tentacles like a living nest of serpents.

We had now reached a plateau. Before us lay some picturesque ruins, which betrayed the hand of man and not that of the Creator. There were vast heaps of stone, amongst which might be traced the vague and shadowy forms of castles, of temples, clothed with a world of flowerlike zoophytes and over which, instead of ivy, seaweed threw a thick vegetable mantle. But what was this region which had been swallowed up by cataclysms? Who had erected those rocks and stones, like the cromlechs of prehistoric times? Where was I? Whither had Captain Nemo hurried me?

I was anxious to ask him; this being impossible, I stopped him – I seized his arm. But shaking his head, and pointing to the crest of mountain he seemed to say—

'Come, come along; come higher!'

I followed, and in a few minutes I had climbed to the top.

I looked down the slope we had just ascended. The mountain did not rise more than seven or eight hundred feet above the plain; but on the far side of the plain it commanded from twice that height the ocean-depths, which were suddenly lit up by a flash like lightning! The mountain was a volcano!

Fifty feet above the peak, in the midst of a rain of stones and volcanic ash, a crater was vomiting forth torrents of lava which fell like a cascade of fire into the surrounding liquid; it lit the plain to the horizon like an immense torch. It threw up lava, but not flames, which require the oxygen of the air and cannot develop under water; but lava can attain a white heat, fight vigorously against the liquid, and transform it into vapour.

Swift currents carried away these gases in diffusion, and torrents of lava rolled to the foot of the mountain like an eruption of Vesuvius. There under my eyes, ruined, destroyed, overthrown, lay a town – its roofs open to the sky, its temples fallen, its arches dislocated, its columns lying on the ground, suggesting the massive character of Tuscan architecture. Further on the remains of a gigantic aqueduct; here the high base of an Acropolis, with the graceful outline of a Parthenon; there the remains of a quay, as if some ancient sea-port with its merchant vessels and its war-galleys had once sheltered on the edge of a long-vanished ocean. Further on again, long lines of sunken walls and broad deserted streets – a second Pompeii swamped beneath the waters.

Where was I? Where was I? I must know at any cost. I tried to speak, I even wanted to wrench off my helmet, but Captain Nemo stopped me by a gesture. Then, picking up a piece of chalk rock, he went up to a slab of black basalt and traced the one word:

ATLANTIS

What a light shot through my mind! Atlantis! the Atlantis of Plato, that continent denied by so many philosophers, believed in by so many others: I had it there before my eyes, bearing witness to its own catastrophe. The region thus engulfed was beyond Europe, Asia and Libya, beyond the pillars of Hercules. Here had lived those powerful people, the Atlanteans, against whom were waged the first wars of ancient Greece. But one night and one day had sufficed to destroy this Atlantis, whose highest summits – the Madeiras, the Azores, the Canaries, and the Cape Verde Islands – still survive.

Thus, led by the strangest destiny, I was treading under foot the mountains of this continent, touching with my hand those ruins a thousand generations old and contemporary with the geological epochs. I was walking on the very spot once trodden by the contemporaries of the first man.

Whilst I was trying to fix in my mind every detail of this mighty landscape, Captain Nemo remained motionless, as though petrified in mute ecstasy, leaning on a mossy stone. Was he dreaming of those generations long since disappeared? Was he asking them the secret of human destiny? Was it here this strange man came to steep himself in historical recollections and live anew this ancient life – he to whom modern life made no appeal? What would I not have given to know his thoughts, to share them, to understand them!

We remained for an hour at this place, contemplating the vast plains under the brightness of the lava, which was at times wonderfully intense. Rapid trembling produced by internal ebullition, convulsed the mountain, loud noises transmitted through the water were echoed with majestic grandeur. Then the moon appeared through the waters and threw her pale rays on the buried continent. It was but a gleam, but how indescribable it effect! The captain rose, cast one last look on that vast plain and signed to me to follow him.

We descended the mountain; then beyond the mineral forest I saw the light of the *Nautilus* shining like a star. The captain walked straight towards her and we boarded her as the first rays of light whitened the surface of the ocean.

[Though it appears in few of his works, the tradition of Ancient Atlantis was obviously one that would appeal greatly

o Verne. He reverted to it towards the end of his life, for it is
rather casually mentioned in the posthumous *Package Holiday,*
and it forms one of the dominant themes in what is believed to
be the very last of his writings, *The Eternal Adam.*

This survey of the development of science fiction thus ends
almost where it began, with strange monsters dwelling in a
realm inimical and normally inaccessible to man, yet with two
heroes moving unafraid among them to revisit the scene of
what may well be an earliest example of science fiction ever
written.]

BIBLIOGRAPHY

SURPRISINGLY little seems to have appeared in Britai[n]
on the development of science fiction. The following works wil[l]
however, be found helpful:

Moore, Patrick, *Science and Fiction* (1957)
Amis, Kingsley, *New Maps of Hell: A Survey of Scienc[e]
    Fiction* (1961)
Green, Roger Lancelyn, *Space Flight in Fiction* (1957)
Nicolson, Marjorie Hope, *Voyages to the Moon* (USA, 1948)
— and Mohler, Nora May, 'The Scientific Background o[f]
    Swift's Voyage to Laputa' and 'Swift's "Flying Island" i[n]
    the Voyage to Laputa' (*Annals of Science,* vol. II, nos 3, [4]
    1957)
De Camp, Lyon Sprague, *Science Fiction Handbook* (USA
    1953)
— and Ley, Willy, *Lands Beyond* (USA, 1952)

*A selection
of recent
Panther Books
is to be found
on the following
pages*

PANTHER BOOKS
presents

THIRTY THOUSAND YEARS OF
GALACTIC HISTORY
with the uniform edition of
ISAAC ASIMOV'S
classic *Foundation* trilogy

FOUNDATION

FOUNDATION AND EMPIRE

SECOND FOUNDATION

each 3/6

'At last, for the first time in Britain,
all three of the *Foundation* books are
available at the same time.

The *Foundation* trilogy is probably the
prime example of "straight" science
fiction published to date. No other
book can compare with the magnificent
scope that this series offers.

For anyone who has not yet read all
three parts I heartily recommend them'

VECTOR
(The Journal of the British Science Fiction Association)

Four pioneering novels by
JULES VERNE
the father of modern science fiction

'His imaginative power is dateless'
KENNETH ALLSOP in
THE DAILY MAIL

'. . . funny, prophetic, biting . . . None
of his novels date; good tale-telling
never does'
TRIBUNE

FIVE WEEKS IN A BALLOON
A classic tale of exploration and peril

BLACK DIAMONDS
A land of dark terror in the bowels
of the earth

PROPELLER ISLAND
They created a floating hell . . . and
called it Utopia

THE SECRET OF WILHELM
STORITZ
He harnessed a fundamental energy of
the Universe that was terrifying in its
implications. . . .
each 3/6

Famous authors in
Panther Books

Henry Miller	Henry Williamson
Norman Mailer	Vladimir Nabokov
Maurice Procter	Fernando Henriques
Jean-Paul Sartre	John O'Hara
Jean Genet	Howard Fast
Alan Moorehead	Hubert Monteilhet
Nicholas Monsarrat	Julian Mitchell
Colin Willock	Agnar Mykle
James Jones	Simon Raven
Erich Maria Remarque	Marcel Proust
Len Deighton	John Rechy
Saki	Gore Vidal
Jack London	John Barth
James Hadley Chase	Alan Williams
Georgette Heyer	Bill Naughton
Rex Stout	John Horne Burns
Isaac Asimov	David Caute
Jules Verne	Ivan Turgenev
Hans Habe	Colin Wilson
Marquis de Sade	H.P.Lovecraft
Doris Lessing	Rachel Carson
Mary McCarthy	Jerzy Peterkiewicz
Edmund Wilson	Curzio Malaparte